BREAKING THE SKY
NO LONGER BOUND
THIS SHOULD NOT BE
YET TRUTH IS FOUND

WYRD WEST

THUNDER ROAD

LUKE TRACEY

Thunder Road

Copyright © Luke Tracey 2025

This is a work of fiction. Names, places, and incidents either are the products of the author's imagination or used fictitiously. No offence is intended toward any living or dead people, beliefs, places, or events.

All rights reserved. No part of this publication may be reproduced, distributed, or transmitted in any form or by any means, including photocopying, recording, or other electronic or mechanical methods, without the prior written permission of the author.

The moral rights of the author are asserted.

Wyrd West created by Luke Tracey.

Published by Phoenix Forge.

ISBN: 978-0-9946426-6-0 (Hardcover)
ISBN: 978-0-9946426-7-7 (Paperback)
ISBN: 978-0-9946426-8-4 (e-Book)

1.2

THUS IS FATE

WYRD WEST

The Civil War is over. Yet, the drive for more of the precious aetron crystal that ended the conflict continues. Hidden forces of the Sicarius Assembly use their influence to increase the push for American expansion into the Wild West, hoping to incite a rush to claim more of the miraculous resource.
Rising against the conquest, the broken natives of Horse Nation and hopeful settlers of Takoda Territory resist the forced assimilation of modern civilization.
Royce Falco, walking the line between both of those worlds, accepts that his growing posse of outlaws may already have their Fate bound to the increasing conflict by an old frontier legend.
That of the Ghost Riders.

THUNDER ROAD

PROLOGUE

WEB OF FATE

Jacobi heard their haunting chorus of voices among the tolling of funeral bells as the nightmarish monster clawed its many limbs and fangs around him.

It was a savage symphony of visceral rhythm, a moment of predacious opportunity when the human prey was claimed and wrenched through the water. Blood flowed from Jacobi's face as each attempted stroke of escape was exchanged for a mouth-full of the river. The collection of scything talons and the watery depths both contended to tear him asunder.

Questions fought their way through Jacobi's excruciating delirium. Had he truly just seen the ghostly riders that belonged to the mournful sounds that had seemed to approach louder and louder again to him alone this night, or were they a figment of his damaged skull? Whatever those spectres were—if that's what they were—they now went unseen, leaving only their mournful cries and the tolling echo of bells as it was before.

There were faint beacons of hope in the distance of the Rubicon River. But, they looked like a hope that was either going to drown with him or a hope that would be torn apart.

Could some of those lights be shining from the *River Grace* that he'd been thrown overboard from? Was that paddle steamer still nearby? Or, perhaps those lights shone from some lonely frontier town?

He couldn't know.

There was no way to know.

The monster had grappled and stabbed at him through the waters far from the steamship he had last stood with dry feet upon.

Jacobi had lost his bearings.

LUKE TRACEY

Of all the lights that he could see, to him it wasn't the starlit night that shone brightest of all against the slicked black of the beast's many limbs or the wafting tendrils of shadowy smoke they seemed formed of.

No, it was the creature's eyes.

So numerous.

So alien.

Each glowed with a scarlet red from within their orbits like the fresh embers of a dying fire. They were slashed with a black pupil reminiscent of a cat's eye, yet the similarities ended there. Instead of one single slit, it was three lines parting equally from the middle.

Gunfire cracked through the chaos as the whips of bullets pierced the water around Jacobi, jarring him from his absolute agony for a quick moment.

The beast's limbs were so many they were without number. When they weren't tendrils of inky smoke, they were like enormous black skeletal fingers protected on one side by a rigid carapace. They responded by attacking with more ferocity, stabbing their blunt-clawed ends like spears in the water.

And when the monster attacked, it emitted a sinister noise from its tri-eyed head, from what may have been a cluster of vicious fangs.

"*Kuhl-kuhl-kuhl...*"

Not always, but often two rapid syllables followed by a longer third.

"Kuhl-kuhl-kuhl..."

Jacobi had no idea how he evaded most of the assault. Something was happening. Some of the attacks slowed, as though time almost stalled, then proceeded normally again.

Whether it was a product of his racing mind or he'd gone insane, he did not know.

The *River Grace* had managed to turn around as best as its paddle-design would allow with what speed its steam engine could give. More shots were fired by rifles from the struggling boat.

The monstrous spider-like beast, at times physical and at others times seemingly ethereal, smashed the water. Human or spider—or something in between—it tried to stir up some cover in an environment that it didn't appear suitable for. It kept its tenuous grasp upon the screaming Jacobi, its massive, knuckled talon-limbs moving him through the flowing river out of reach from the paddle steamer. Again, with each spluttered breath of more-water-than-air, he thought this would be his end.

"Kuhl-kuhl-kuhl..."

The arachnid monster—because, to Jacobi, a spider is what this hulking man-thing was most reminiscent of—sunk its array of fangs into Jacobi's neck. A tail thrashed in the water, at times trying to steady its prey and at others trying to propel the beast.

Those many crimson orbs it used to see leered so close. It had a skull, a head adorned with sets of those tri-slitted eyes, with a swooping carapace atop it that separated rearward like some kind of three-horned devil.

There was a strange exchange.

"Kuhl-kuhl-kuhl..."

The eyes—so many of them—shone a brighter red. He didn't know how, but by some means Jacobi saw that there were nine of those baleful orbs. Three to a set. More eyes than any ordinary-sized spider he knew of should have.

Something moved through the fangs into him...but it was more of a feeling, an emotion, thoughts...than some sort of venom.

And in return, something of Jacobi...something of himself went back through those fangs into the nightmare that beset him.

The nine eyes and the clutch of fangs worked in concert, wispy tendrils of black bleeding about into the chaotic air. The fangs...more than two—three? It felt as though more than two gripped his neck.

Darkness overtook Jacobi followed by waking every few moments.

As the steamer's paddle wheel spun furiously, cutting into the river for speed, Jacobi managed to struggle around enough from the beast to see a handful of *River Grace* security guards firing their rifles from the parapet of the upper deck.

Jacobi's idiot friend—the very reason he was overboard—was among the gawking onlookers. He couldn't be sure, but he thought he may have also glimpsed the mysterious card playing magician he'd encountered moving among them. With a little hope, the Gold Baroness wouldn't be there, the sizable poker table debt to her perhaps rescinded after he was cast overboard? The relief of potentially escaping that debt sure didn't outweigh the visceral pain of the unexpected escape provided by Jacobi's friend. That moron had started pointing and shouting drunken commands as though he was somehow helping to fix the situation that he had caused.

While most bullets just found water, one did strike the monster—a green blood spilling on the river. Another cut through the outer flesh of Jacobi's left arm—spilling like a red cloud into the water.

Jacobi had a split-second of intense clarity to wonder what sort of rescue attempt the *River Grace* was hoping to accomplish by shooting at both the predator and the prey.

In response, the arachnidan beast released Jacobi. But as it did, silk strands shot from hidden places inside the array of fangs. The sinuous scythe-like legs spun him, weaving the available webbing around him into a partial shroud.

"Kuhl-kuhl-kuhl…"

The monster fled toward the riverbank, but hauled its unfinished cocoon behind, never relinquishing the human quarry. It evaded the bullets with a preternatural awareness, changing course while submerging and remerging with splashed cover to cause confusion as to its location.

Jacobi's life somehow held on. He felt as though he was being crushed inside the partial cocoon of sticky silver silk as he coughed blood against some of the water and webbing inside his throat.

Breaking the carnage, there was a crack of thunder and before the noise had echoed away, the spectral riders that Jacobi thought he had seen when falling overboard had returned.

They were cowboys on flaming horses materialising into existence in the night sky from some broken rift, a storm formed of heavy wind, scattering rain, swooping blackbirds and a swallowing darkness. The spectres circled above the thrashing arachnid as though the beast was carrion. They were wraithlike with the corvids, their phantom horses flying without wings.

Amidst their ghostly numbers was a barbarian, formed of dark fire with feathers in his wild hair, riding a great bird. Each beat of the giant creature's wings sounded with thunder in time with the tolling of bells while flashes of lightning shot from its eyes. The storming beats resounded among the immaterial horses' sparking hooves and their rider's sombre dirges.

Upon the winged storm, the savage raised a bow formed of antlers and pulled back on an arrow, aiming at the monstrous arachnid. River water parted into waves as the massive electric bird sped close through the air over it.

The many-legged monster altered its course, unrelenting, when the arrow bounced from a dark knuckled limb.

The river gave way again, but to smaller bulging waves like opening mouths of water. Huge alligators, like dragons from old tales, as black as night with their armoured scales slick, came at Jacobi. But they approached not to fight for a torn morsel of the prey, but instead passed him by. They appeared to be working in unison, that preternatural awareness showing again, almost like they were trying to protect Jacobi's predator and distract its attackers.

The spectres rode through the air with the blackbirds alongside the barbarian rider as though there were stable ground beneath the sparking and scorching hooves of their phantom steeds. They fired rusted revolvers with bullets of hellfire and threw lasso loops of burning steel at the monsters as the corvids cawed insults.

The savage drew another arrow from nothingness, pulled back upon a bow string formed of wind, releasing it as a stroke of lightning toward the monstrous spider-thing.

Jacobi heard the frightful riders singing a terrifying tune during a waking moment, so very reminiscent of the distant voices he couldn't place earlier, but to his ears it now sounded with the clarity of an unwanted requiem among the bells that still tolled.

Was this his time to die?

The monster arachnid wouldn't give up its bound prize, but neither would the ghostly riders on the storm.

Another arrow of lightning finally freed Jacobi from being towed by the giant spider, releasing him to roll partially cocooned onto the wet riverside. The bolt had struck the beast in one of its scarlet eyes, the monster screeching with a shrill defiance.

The black alligators withdrew. They scattered to the depths, submerging, swallowed by the river.

LUKE TRACEY

Under the once starry night, the giant arachnid-thing scurried into the trees of the river foreshore, surrounded by a mist of inky vapour. The monster was followed by the ghostly hunters and swirling blackbirds within their storm into the woods.

When the fiery barbarian came for him upon those thundering wings, the gravely brutalised Jacobi passed out once more.

PART I

FALL FROM GRACE

CHAPTER

ONE

When Jacobi regained consciousness, the sun was shining bright. From which direction, he couldn't tell. As for the rest of the world, that all appeared to be moving away from his bare feet.

The moment didn't make a lick of sense.

As he began to regain more control of his wits and his eyes adjusted to the glare a little, he realised that he was resting upon some form of stretcher that was supported by two long poles dragging their ends in the earth.

On a bed. That dragged. Moving.

Jacobi was on his back, angled head above feet. Something was pulling the contraption along behind his head, away from the direction he faced: so, he was moving away from the world that he could see, not the other way around.

An unfamiliar kind of bird flew by, joining others with song upon the branches of a tree that he also didn't recognise. The tune was harmonious music compared to the memory of wailing moans and crow-calls that were clawing their way back from somewhere deep in his memory.

The mental discomfort was enough to force himself to shift to try to look around.

Jacobi's body was wrapped in various bloodied rags, some of them appearing to be torn from what was left of his own clothing. He recognised the material of his vest, torn into many of the wraps, as were his lower trousers. His shirt was practically useless, the shreds just waving about providing minor cover from the sun. Pain was beginning to spread the more he studied himself, the casual examination by eye being a reminder to the rest of his damaged body to catch up to his waking mind.

Although he was fastened to this makeshift moving stretcher, he wasn't tied down in such a fashion that he thought he was a prisoner.

But if he wasn't somebody's prisoner, was he somebody's patient?

Jacobi was becoming bewildered; everything just adding up to too much at once. Combined with the rising pain, memories started flooding back and his world went black.

He heard them. Again.

As though lost voices trailed on a wind accompanied by a rhythmic beat. Like a faint chorus from Beyond.

"Jacobi!"

The interruption struck like a sting, pulling away his efforts to focus on what could only be described as otherworldly.

"Another beer?"

It was his idiot friend: Francis.

Or for full effect: Francis Geddes, the Idiot Friend.

That irritating voice could find him even in other rooms. It cut through the haze of stranger voices and sounds that he was actually trying to concentrate upon over the normal lively hum of the room.

If Francis could just give him a single moment of peace.

Francis and Jacobi were on board the *River Grace,* a luxurious paddle steamer that promised the thrill of high-stakes gambling while taking in the sights of the wild western frontier on the Rubicon River. The steamer departed the modern city of La Grande on the river's east side, climbing the map northward, destined to find port in the logging town of Rosewood on the river's west side after a few weeks of travel.

Jacobi's face fell into his hands at the poker table as he released a frustrated sigh. Francis was calling for him from out of eyesight again, loud enough to offend other patrons that spoke at a more subdued level.

And somehow, that idiot Francis had landed them in trouble. Again.

More than trouble, though.

Bordering on actual danger this time.

LUKE TRACEY

Seated across the poker table from Jacobi was Charles Lafayette, twizzling his curling moustache. He was a mysterious man whose verbose claims included his profession to be that of a travelling magician. Unlike the other gentlemen on board, the magician didn't remove his hat indoors, and it was as though the overly-wide midnight blue brim created more of a shadow upon his face than it reasonably should have.

Each time the magician's hypnotic gaze met his eyes through that shady veil, Jacobi caught sound of those distant voices again, sounding like they were wailing from outside the confines of the steamer. Occasionally, there was the cawing of a bird with it, but it too was difficult to place.

He dared not ask anyone if they also heard the inexplicable chorus for fear of being branded with lunacy. It seemed very apparent that nobody else heard these things.

He was alone with these strange noises.

One time, as Jacobi did his best to not appear as peculiar as he felt while listening to the mysterious sounds, he attempted to mimic the weird way the magician rearranged the cards of his poker hand. It was his hope that this would calm his anxiousness and help him to better blend in at the table.

Turns out it didn't help at all.

After the new arrangement, Jacobi swore the playing cards in his hand burst into flames! The club and spade suits became bells and skulls. But as quickly as he witnessed the ignition, and before he could raise alarm, the cards had returned to their previous pristine state. The original suits were there on the fronts and the *River Grace* logo remained uncharred on their backside. No evidence of the bizarre combustion or changing suits remained on the cards.

Not even a sniff of ash in the air.

Still trying to keep his composure under the strange duress, Jacobi looked around the table at the others seated. It only seemed as though the flare of the cards had caught the magician's attention.

Jacobi wondered if Charles Lafayette could also hear the mysterious voices. Was it worth asking? But then, was this all perhaps just a cheap carnival trick of the magician?

Somewhere, a bird cawed again.

CHAPTER

TWO

What...what just happened?

Almost as if to answer his confusion with more confusion, a dog with a thick fur coat slowed its walk to match pace with the wounded human. At first Jacobi witnessed a much smaller stretcher packed with sundries slow down beside him until it eventually slowed enough that the dog hauling it could be seen.

Jacobi's heartbeat had skipped when he thought for a split-second that it was a wolf! But this had to be simply a dog with volumes of red and white fur that was very similar.

Right? Similar...wasn't it?

THUNDER ROAD

Jacobi didn't really know much about such things. Wolves weren't common knowledge back home and he hadn't read up on them before leaving. He was usually stuck in the pages of fiction rather than fact.

Especially dime novels. He loved those.

The dog was, thankfully, cheerful with its tongue panting and tail wagging. At least, where Jacobi was from, he knew enough about dogs to know it was a good sign. The animal studied him with curiosity from eyes of two different colours. One of blue and the other brown. Jacobi swore the dog was trying to smile at him as it pulled its own load of trappings along the same worn dirt path as whatever was dragging him in the stretcher.

He still couldn't comprehend what he was seeing, adding the shock of a potential wolf mauling onto it. Mixed with all that was going on with the pain and confusion, his disoriented mind simply switched off again, passing into unconscious as he wondered if this was what it was like when your life was supposed to flash before your eyes.

On the other side of the dealer to the magician, smoking a fat cigar, was the owner of the M.M.C..

The Matthias Mining Consortium.

This was where the trouble Francis had gotten them into really was.

Twyla Matthias would pronounce her, "Double-Emm-See," organisation with the same tone of pride as someone patriotically referring to the U.S.A.. Her sinister boasting as the *Gold Baroness of the Wild West* would place emphasis on the rhyming of *Baroness* and *West*.

Adding to her demeanour and modes of speech, the endless supplies of money and the pair of personal *River Grace* staff bodyguards standing nearby all cast her as an extremely dangerous woman.

But there was also something odd about her that Jacobi couldn't place. Something *wrong* with her...

With her outline.

Her shadow.

Sometimes it was like it stood behind her, and other times it was as though it stood away as another's shadow. It was almost as though her shadow was someone else...or some-*thing* else. And like the noises and cards, Jacobi was sure he was the only one experiencing it.

Was there something in the beer here?

Francis made a meandering return with another two bottles of the stuff in hand. Some foam spilled from the necks to his hands, causing him to sample both on the way by means of trying to clean the mess with his tongue.

Another sigh. Francis at his best.

The Gold Baroness was very interested in the young man's answer as to where he was going to get the money owed to her. Money that he had said that he and Jacobi would, "Be good for."

Twyla closed her bejewelled gold pocket watch—not so much because she had been looking at the time on one side or using the mirror to check her flawless skin on the other, but more to flaunt her excessive wealth as a continued display of power.

Power...that elicited fear.

"Francis and Jacobi from Boston, Massachusetts..." She spoke deliberately, annunciating disbelief in Francis' previous tales by pushing the last syllables of their place of origin so hard that it almost sounded like a snake hissing. "Two dandy Boston boys travel westward because one of them is about to be married to the other's sister. One big adventure before tying the knot. But they find fortune along the way in Boom Town, prospecting claims enough to buy ranches and cattle. Suddenly wealthy cowboys...a fairy tale as old and told and sold as time. A tale that you'd write to your bride-to-be about Back East. But you boys don't have enough on hand to pay your way out of a very bad hand of poker, not even a handful of gold dust or a hint of crushed aetron from your fortuitous prospecting?"

Twyla pushed her gold-rimmed spectacles closer to her face, peering over her piles of winnings. Francis and Jacobi saw their worried faces reflected on the glasses. "I happen to know a thing or two about gold and aetron, and how to obtain it. You see boys, my busy schedule sees me travelling for pleasure on this ship to Rosewood. Then I'll be meeting some business associates in Sundown. Then I'll be making the long journey to Boom Town, where I have a few operations. Problem is, I've never heard of you two. But, according to my guards here," she thumbed over her shoulder at her uniformed enforcers, "the *River Grace's* register has you listed as one Francis Geddes and one Jacobi Nicholson, from Boston, Massachusetts, lodging in private single cabin numbers thirteen and three, respectively. Two dandies from Boston, that I assume don't have the frontier experience required to have ever travelled westward enough to reach Boom Town. Two dandies from Boston that now owe me five hundred and seventy-nine dollars and fifty-five cents…"

"Well, we, uh," Francis spilled beer on his floral-patterned vest as he put the other bottle down on the table with a drunk hand in front of his friend. Getting back into his chair with clumsy poise, Francis then knocked that bottle and the bowl of nuts beside it into Jacobi's lap, "we uh…"

"Frann-siss!" Jacobi stood up, trying to wipe away some of the dampness.

He'd had enough.

"Excuse us a moment, *Gentlemen*, *Lady*. I need to have a serious talk to my…fu…*friend*." He grabbed Francis by the scruff of his shirt, "Come on," leading him away.

Jacobi had managed to ignore the haunting wails and occasional bird squawk for most of Twyla's tirade. If anything, he was fixated upon her strange shifting shadow. But, those haunting sounds were rising in volume again. Becoming more difficult to ignore.

Twyla's uniformed thugs moved to intercept, but she waved for them to allow the Boston boys to leave. "They'll be back. Will you not, boys? Besides, we're surrounded by a whole lot of river. The *Ragin' Rubicon River*. One of the biggest in the world. So with that much water, where else but this steamboat could you possibly go?"

CHAPTER

THREE

Jacobi woke to the world again and wrestled with the bindings that were keeping him from falling out of his slanted bed. He loosened them enough to have a better look around, increasing his agony.

He tried to cast his mind back to what happened before now. He touched his face to a stinging response, pressing upon some sort of fixing covering the wound.

Perhaps, the smashed bottle from onboard the *River Grace...*?

He had wrapped injuries from cuts and punctures along his ribs and arms and around his neck.

He had been mauled by some giant spider-thing in that river...bitten and cocooned and dragged.

But the monster was more than that.

It was like some sort of person, able to stand upright, but merged as one with a spider. Combined. But armoured around skeletal-like limbs that bled a hazy black mist. And those eyes. The sort of nightmare you'd find in scary books or hard-to-find cartoon strips.

None of it made any sense.

The spider-thing was like a waking dream, the images slowly slipping away from memory with each second.

He wasn't exactly travelling in any form of luxury that would help his predicament. Laying down, his patched head was high enough that even in his groggy state, he could see down his bandaged and padded body to his shoeless feet and the trail left behind that had led through a forested area.

How odd. His feet and legs were almost the only uninjured part of his body.

Jacobi could hear a chant in a language that he didn't recognise. That seemed to be the theme since he journeyed westward and stepped on that paddle steamer: hearing mysterious songs beyond his understanding. Thankfully, it was nothing like the deathly chorus that he had recently experienced. Instead, this sounded more joyous.

More...*alive*.

And going back, what were they? Those ghostly riders. Like the monster, had they even been real? Had any of it been real?

He forced his neck to turn against protesting muscles and wound dressings. He saw the rear buckskin flanks of a horse with loaded saddlebags dragging his stretcher.

The horse's rider sensed Jacobi's movement and looked back to face him. Rumpled hat with feather, long dark hair underneath that was also decorated with a feather, and a face like...

Like...dark fire.

It was the barbarian from upon the gigantic thundering bird!

An *Indian*. An actual American Indian!

But, again, did all that really happen, with the ghostly riders, the thundering bird, and the nine-eyed spider? And there were those alligators too. He had been dragged through river water toward his death and his recollection was like some bad dream.

THUNDER ROAD

Delirium? Nightmare?

If these memories were simply a bad dream, some insane nightmare, the all-too-real wounds would certainly disagree.

And now the barbarian was riding a horse and wearing clothes no different to any other person he'd seen while travelling closer to the western frontier with Francis.

And Francis—his idiot friend.

What had become of Francis?

Jacobi winced, his head throbbing. It was all starting to overwhelm him again. Too much.

Not again, he thought, *just stay awake*.

The Indian met Jacobi's trying gaze with a smile, nodded, and tipped his hat with a quick salute of two fingers from the brim. "Welcome back..."

Perhaps not, was Jacobi's last thought, overwhelmed with pain and confusion as his world faded to black again.

Jacobi snatched their boater hats from a pair of hooks near an exit door of the gambling parlours, guiding his stumbling *friend* outside into the night.

He grasped the outer railing with white knuckles at the edge of the paddle steamer, too angry to take in the splendour of the starlit American Frontier across the river's edge. Jacobi turned on Francis. "You always do this, Francis. You never shut up. And you land us in the most ridiculous situations. I can't stand it!"

Jacobi was livid.

After years of Francis getting on his nerves, he was ready to break. "We owe, big time! Because you're the one who kept making stupid bets on stupid hands. And I have to save you. I have to always feel sorry for you. Over five hundred dollars. She sounds like a crime boss. Not the ones in books, but a real one. Do you know what they do to people like us? You're an idiot and you just don't stop!"

Francis took a sip of what was left of his beer, attempting to think. He then pushed Jacobi. "I don't much like the way you're talkin' to me."

"Well, I don't like talking to you at all. Never really have. I got stuck with you and your family after my parents died and somehow I am forced into marrying your sister. You are just always there." Jacobi pushed him back. "And I *just* wish you would *just* shut your trap for *just* five minutes!"

Francis managed to slap the boater hat off from the top of Jacobi's head, sending it spinning overboard like a tossed pie plate. "Don't bring Gertie into this."

Jacobi wasn't known to swear. "Fugg you, Francis, you stupid idiot!" But he'd reached his limit.

He took both stupid sides of stupid Francis' stupid boater hat, lifted it off his stupid head, then pulled the stupid thing down so hard that Francis' stupid reddish head of stupid hair popped through the stupid ribboned lid from the stupid inner brim, leaving only the stupid empty circle of what remained of the stupid brim resting around his stupid neck on his stupid shoulders. "You've had that coming for years, you *stupid* idiot!"

Francis returned the gesture with a wild swing of his beer bottle across Jacobi's face, liquor and shattering glass falling about the deck.

This managed to finally get the attention of a few of the *River Grace* guards on deck.

There was no way that Jacobi was going to be able to respond. His world turned upside-down, spinning, blood flowing from the gash presenting on his face. As he tried to keep hold of the boat's rail and remain conscious, he could hear those eerie voices again, rising, almost singing, alongside an approaching rumble.

An approaching storm.

Somewhere, a church bell tolled and a bird cawed in response. It was only for Jacobi's ears, and he knew it was a funeral bell sounding as though struck for when someone dies.

In his drunken stupor, Francis shoved the disoriented Jacobi onto the guard rail. "You ungrateful, Fugger. After everything my family has done for you."

Francis heaved Jacobi over...

As he peered over the edge, his intoxication rendering him unable to perceive the magnitude of what he had just done, Francis declared, "Perhaps a splash in the river will sorry you up a bit, Jacobi."

The *River Grace's* security approached too late. They caught Francis passing out from excessive inebriation and attempted to wake him.

Different bells clanged from different directions at different times. The alarm bells of the *River Grace* and those otherworldly chimes sounded together, but not in unison.

Jacobi heard the beating rhythm of thundering hooves intensify, accompanied by the wailing choir of voices raised among the bells. Birds cawed as though fighting over a fresh kill.

As he fell from the *River Grace* toward the depths of the Rubicon River, Jacobi caught sight of ghostly riders upon ethereal horses flying through an unnatural storm full of black birds that had broken the previously tranquil starlit night sky.

But more sinister than that imagery, something menacing clung from the side of the steamer's hull, half submerged by the passing river.

Something far more sinister.

A creature that was both spider-like and man-like, formed of mist and shadow that almost wasn't there. With limbs that held preternaturally to the hull, the monster had too many glowing red eyes gazing upon its falling human prey.

PART II

GOING WEST

CHAPTER

FOUR

The appetising aroma from a small pot hanging over the crackling campfire woke Jacobi from his fitful slumber. The smell was unlike anything he'd ever experienced before.

"Would you like some coffee?"

The Bostonian startled, but then calmed.

The voice was strong, but gentle.

It was the same voice that had been chanting a foreign song in one of his previous waking moments.

Jacobi hadn't realised that the barbarian from his overboard nightmare—the Indian that seemingly rescued him—was just nearby preparing something from the metal pot hanging above the fire.

"It, uh..." Jacobi was hesitant, "doesn't smell like coffee..."

He was unsure how safe he was around a *Savage of the Wild West*. While travelling with Francis—and even before they had departed Boston!—the terrible tales of vicious Indians grew worse the farther westward they reached. Robbing wagons, stealing from locomotives, rustling horses, attacking settlers, fighting the Army.

The list went on.

But the most terrifying...

Scalping strangers.

Scalping foreigners like them—tourists!

The Indian smiled, almost chuckling. He wasn't covered in warpaint or an abundance of feathers and beads as the stories and some photographs had told. "This could be the best coffee you have ever had...if I do say so myself." He came over, handing a metal mug to Jacobi, long dark hair falling straight about a leather vest. "It may also help with your snoozing problem."

The dog was there, following with great interest as it watched the mug exchange from weathered tan hand to injured pale fingers. Ever present, the red dog that could be mistaken for a wolf circled around until it found sniffing Jacobi's wound dressings more exciting.

He couldn't see the Indian's horse, but its baggage and sundries were nearby. The bed Jacobi woke upon—level with the ground this time—was made of all the fixings that were once the dragged stretcher.

But Jacobi's pillow, that was the Indian's horse saddle. What an odd, but kind, gesture.

They were among trees that were densely grown enough to almost provide an enclosed camp. The Indian returned to an area of gathered firewood. He resumed fashioning something of branches, twine and fur.

With caution, Jacobi tasted the hot beverage. He already trusted this man more than he would have a normal stranger—whatever *normal* may be considered westward of the Rubicon. But he still retained some wariness.

"This is nothing like Boston coffee!" A wondrous sensation filled him as the hot brew slid over his tongue, as though half his wounds gave up complaining in exchange for the pleasure of the fluid filling his body. "It's amazing—what's your secret?"

"Eggshells," was the answer followed by a wry smile, "and *Indian* magic."

Jacobi didn't know what to make of that as he sipped more of the delicious brew.

"If it helps you stay awake longer," the Indian nodded to the coffee, "you'll be able to eat something, which will help with healing. I'll be cooking some grits soon."

"Grits...?"

The Indian only answered with a smile.

Jacobi's wounded muscles twinged across his back, but to a lesser degree than earlier. He did feel hunger, but it was like it couldn't be bothered to present itself properly in his condition.

"Pardon my asking, but I'm guessing that's not a wolf. Is it a dog?" He hoped he was offering the right question as the guardedness that remained reminded him that he still didn't know how safe he was.

Was Jacobi prisoner or patient?

"You refer to Rusty?" The Indian then shook his head. "He's only a wolf in spirit." Then he tapped his chest with a gentle fist. "We do not...the People...my people...the

Horse Nation...we do not make much of a distinction. He's not a wolf as you may understand it. Breeders of the Great White North and beyond call his kin, *husky*. Some call him by the name *Dog*, while the few that know him call him by a handful of names. But friends...friends, they call him *Rusty*."

Jacobi ran what few undamaged fingers he had through the thick red and white fur upon the agreeable animal. "*Rusty*...not the sort of name I was expecting from a..."

His rescuer raised an eyebrow like he'd heard it all before. "An Indian?"

"Well, simply put, yes...from you. I confess I know very little of this world I've landed in."

"One that admits he knows little will learn much..."

"I hope so." Jacobi didn't mean to cause any offence, and it looked as though none was taken. "Was it an obvious choice, naming him?"

The Indian became lost in thought for a moment, recalling some old memories of the dog. "My Brother has a penchant for naming people, places, things, animals. *Rusty* was the only name that worked, so it stuck."

"He's very friendly."

"He does not usually accept strangers so soon like that—he must see a kindness in your spirit." The Indian looked fondly at the cheerful dog. "Those that cross him...I have seen men in worse situations in Rusty's jaws than when you were ensnared by that monster."

That took Jacobi by surprise.

"Speaking of that," Jacobi wanted—needed—to know more about the monster. "There's so much I don't know."

The Indian mentioning the creature brought the memories to a fuller state of factuality, a place in his mind where he could accept that the events after falling overboard really had occurred.

"I've had a night that tops all nights. I'm sure you won't believe me...well, except for the monster at the end. It started with haunting voices. Approaching, like some old ghost story. Then when I rearranged my poker hand—fwoosh!" Jacobi re-enacted the motions. "The cards burst into flames. The suits changed. Then they weren't on fire. And then they were back to normal. This magician wearing a big blue hat, Charles Lafayette his name was, he seemed the only one to notice."

The Indian's eyes widened and a little smirk crept across his lips at the mention of the magician before his facial features resumed their resting stoic expression.

Jacobi's telling was gaining speed, caused by the apprehension of reliving the memories. "My idiot friend, Francis...we had a fight because he got us into debt with the *Gold Baroness of the Wild West* who probably would have killed us before we made final port in Rosewood."

Alarm rose in Hawk's eyes with the mention of the Gold Baroness. "Or, more likely," the Indian interrupted, "she would have made you slaves in Boom Town to work off your debt. That could be considered almost the same as death."

"She can't do that?" Jacobi was shocked. "Can she?"

"While there is a difference between what we may see as what is right and what is wrong, there is also what those in power permit themselves to do when there is no authority to guide them...or worse, when they are the authority."

"Well, she did say she was going from Rosewood to Sundown to Boom Town." Jacobi was facing many challenges in this West, including some moral philosophies that differed from back home. "I guess I avoided slavery, because, then Francis ended up knocking me overboard with that monster, that spider-thing...and then I see—well, first, what were those other *things* in the water with it? What was any of it?"

The Indian absorbed Jacobi's words before answering. "For generations, the people of Mudflats have called those monstrous beasts: *Terrorgators.*"

"So they're some type of alligator?"

"Perhaps, but that all depends on your perception. They are not like any common alligator. There are stories told, most of it forgotten over the years or remembered as myth or superstition. But as you know it, it is as real as you and I speaking to each other about it now."

"Like that giant spider-thing. That was no myth either! What was that?"

"A nightmare perhaps beyond your current understanding. There are many mysteries in these lands, and not everyone can see them—or chooses to see them."

While he wasn't getting a proper answer about the spider-monster, Jacobi thought that the Indian's grasp of the English language was superb. It wasn't the broken American English he'd been told that only a scant few Indians could manage. "And speaking of seeing things, that brings me to another matter. I can't even believe what I'm about to say, so pardon me when I ask..."

Jacobi swallowed.

"Who...or what...were those cowboys that rode through the sky?"

The Indian stopped his crafting. "Cowboys?"

"Those hellish cowboys that rode through the storm in the sky on horses around you, bells tolling, dirges wailing, crows and ravens squawking—it's enough to drive someone insane. Were they ghosts? Have I seen ghosts? You can't have not seen it, or heard it, you were there..."

"I was," the Indian replied with a raised brow.

"But you weren't like this," Jacobi twirled a finger at the Indian, "as you are now...you rode on a gigantic storming bird ahead of the cowboys, all of you riding after me and those monsters in the river."

"There were no other riders. I was upon horseback, coming for you among those monsters. Rusty was back at the camp, guarding."

"Fugg me!" Jacobi pressed the dressing on his face. "Excuse my cussing, but I really must have been out of sorts."

The Indian stood, trying to mask his obvious astonishment at hearing the tales. "I rode after the monsters that sought you, in particular the beast that had you, my arrows unable to find their mark. I was trying to force it to release you. It would have cocooned you in its web and fed on your broken body and spirit."

As Jacobi turned a lighter shade of pale, his rescuer became very solemn as though he accepted some sort of truth. "But, perhaps the Trikuhl wished a Fate worse than your death..."

"*Try...cull*—is that what the giant spider-man-thing is called?"

"Only to the handful of us that know better."

"But tell me, what could actually be worse than a giant spider eating you?" Jacobi's skin went impossibly paler again. "It was some good luck that you were there! I had bad luck at the poker table before I went overboard, but it was good luck that you came along."

The Indian nodded to himself, pondering Jacobi's words. "I have been tracking many monsters these past winters, or years as you would count them. Things that civilised folk refuse to believe exist. Yet it is the worst sort of monster, though, when they are actually human—for it is only their atrocities that are difficult to believe. One monster led me on the trail to a second, a human monster that I have been tracking for many years. A cruel woman that you encountered."

"The Gold Baroness of the Wild West?"

"The same. Twyla Matthias."

Jacobi's eyes widened as the Indian returned to his crafting.

"As you know," the Indian explained, "she was on your paddle steamer."

"Yes! She's why I fell overboard. Well, Francis, the idiot I was travelling with, managed to get us into debt for over five hundred dollars to her. Francis and I had a fight over it—and, wow, did he have it coming!—and, as you know, I didn't come out of it so well."

"I was following your boat along the shore when I heard the commotion in the water, so I went to investigate. Eventually, those on the steamer started firing their guns, as they often do when panicked by something they don't understand. I loosed arrows at the Trikuhl, hoping the steamboat's rifles would handle the Terrorgators."

"That's when those devilish riders were there in the sky, wailing, bells and birds and storms hammering on, going after the monsters with you, and you shot the spider-thing in the eye with an arrow of lightning while they fired their flaming guns and threw red-hot ropes."

"I was riding alone, there were no others."

Jacobi had become so sure of what he had witnessed with each time he spoke of it. "I'm telling you; they were cowboys from Hell, on flying flaming steeds...and they were like...like death...like they were dead...some with fiery skulls and some with sunken faces...and you were at their lead, riding a great bird made of storm and thunder and shooting lightning...Fugg! I can't believe what I'm saying, but I know what I saw. It's become so vivid."

The Indian didn't respond for a moment after that. Jacobi had never seen a man go so deep into thought before. He thought Francis deciding between eating liquorice or rock candy took severe concentration, but this was at another level above that.

"So, who are you," the Indian finally asked, locking eyes with sincerity, "he that can shuffle flaming cards, and sees and hears ghostly riders with corvids and tolling bells and thundering birds and veiled monsters?"

CHAPTER

FIVE

"Nobody." The Bostonian tourist didn't know any other way to answer. "I mean, that, I'm nobody important...my name is Jacobi..."

"Only Jacobi? White men usually carry more names than that."

"Jacobi Nicholson. From Boston, Massachusetts."

The Indian came over to Jacobi and pulled excess blankets from him. "If you feel you are a prisoner, Jacobi Nicholson from Boston, Massachusetts, you are not. You are free. We should always be free."

Jacobi felt assured that he wasn't a prisoner.

"What do I call you?" He tried to stand, not knowing how many days it had been since he had last used his legs.

The Indian had brought his crafting over and raised it before Jacobi: a walking crutch constructed from strong branches bound in entwined sinew and reeds with a fur underarm support. There was a feather and some beads hanging from it.

As he pulled Jacobi to his shaky feet, he placed the crutch under his aching armpit to help him stand and replied, "Which do you want to know? The name I was given at my birth, the name I grew up with, the name the white men made me choose, the name I chose for myself...? There are many."

"That's...a lot of names, but whichever one you like the most, the one you go by now." Jacobi thought a moment. "The name I would come to say to you as a friend, like I would say to Rusty."

The Indian smiled at the dog, reflecting. "Now you are making new friends for me?"

Rusty circled, tail wagging with a joyful response.

"In your tongue, people who come to know me, call me..." It seemed for a second that the Indian had to think about what his name was, as though he was about to speak one word but released another. "Hawk."

"Like the bird?"

"With regard to saying it, yes."

Jacobi tried it. "*Hawk...*"

Then he offered, "Sometimes, people that can't be bothered don't call me Jacobi; they call me Jack."

"*Shev...*" Hawk answered, as though he had to sum the word up from deep within.

"I don't know what that means."

"In the tongue of the People—my people, the Takoda of the Horse Nation—that is what you would call me. *Shev* is what my people call me."

"Thank you for helping me...*Hawk*, for saving me." Though it caused him visible pain, Jacobi extended a hand toward the Indian, "Thank you, *Shev*...my new friend in this Wild West."

Rusty interrupted with a gentle bark.

"Of course, you too, Rusty," Jacobi added with a smile.

The Indian stood there for a second, staring at the reaching hand. "Forgive my hesitation. My people must often fight the learned notion that such a gesture is often accompanied with deceit."

But Hawk accepted the handshake.

"You are welcome, *Jacobi* Nicholson of Boston, Massachusetts. This is how we become. *Jack* of the Wild West. *Thus is Fate.*"

"I guess it is…" Jacobi didn't really understand fate. Well, not in the way that his new friend probably did. Religion and dime novels had only explained so much to Jacobi. He still pondered the meaning, though, as he looked around the camp.

It appeared to be relatively packed away in wooden boxes and trunks, almost ready to move, with wrapped furs and skins piled on top. "Pardon me, Hawk, but after all of this…if I am to go, are you able to tell me which way to go?"

Hawk nodded. "I would travel with you, but now that you are healing I must devote my attention elsewhere. One of the few white men I trust should be arriving today to pack the camp and take the goods I have crafted for sale. I will ask him to take you and teach you how to find your friend and how to find your way home. The West is no place for the unprepared."

"Oh, I'm done with Francis," Jacobi explained. "If this is how fate works, *how we become*, as you say, then fate did me a favour. Francis'll still be afloat on that boat as it paddles on without me. Hopefully he thinks I'm dead. I'm sure they had to give up on me eventually. I never have to see that idiot or his family again—or return east for that matter."

"You don't want to return home?"

Jacobi shook his head. "My parents died when I was young. The black lung. I had no brothers or sisters. I was taken in by the Geddes family. A constant hassle to live with. Forced to be best friends with the son. Forced to soon marry the daughter. Forced to be smothered by the mother. Forced to work for the father. There was no escape—until now."

Hawk absorbed the situation. "As I said earlier, no person should feel like they are a prisoner."

"That's exactly what I was. One of those situations I was born into...my fate. The whole reason I wanted to go West was because I was always drawn this way to escape. From rumours to cheap story books to newspaper articles, everything I read spoke to me, told me that I was going westward one day. Being betrothed to Gertrude Geddes was going to take that away from me when the Big Day came. So as one last adventure before marriage, Francis and I decided to travel the Wild West we'd heard so much about. Sure there was a lot of opposition to us going, but it was the one fight I stood my ground on. Francis only came along because...well, Francis is like a bug you just can't flick off. I never felt like I belonged in Boston with the Geddes. That place, the people, their ideas for my life, it wasn't me, and I wanted to be somewhere else...to be someone else. Can we alter fate? As far as I'm concerned, I am free...finally free...more free than I have ever been in my life. I hope that all makes sense to you."

Jacobi motioned over his wounds. "Look at me. If this is what it costs to get out, then it was worth it." He was more lucid than he'd been since the steamboat incident.

Was it the coffee working its apparent magic or the elation of lost shackles and new beginnings...perhaps both?

"The old Jacobi fell overboard from the *River Grace* and may as well have been eaten by that monstrous spider in the Rubicon

River. One could say, *rest in peace*, Jacobi Nicholson, from Boston, Massachusetts. Your time is up. And welcome to *Jack*. But my journey isn't over because I fell off that boat, thanks to you. I've seen too much that people—to use a phrase I've heard here a few times—*Back East* wouldn't believe. So, I promise you, this Jacobi, this Jack, is going to continue to Go West."

There was something in the way Jacobi's mock-eulogy and new determination about Fate affected Hawk, as though he was struck with the awe of a welcomed epiphany.

"Take this," the Indian reached into his vest and pulled some sort of necklace with a charm from around his head, "keep it with you along your new journey."

"What is it?" Jacobi held the strange ornament of the necklace aloft by its leather strings, studying the intricate wood carving, a long white feather hanging from it. It occupied his attention in a way that he'd never experienced before. He was drawn to the pendant, like he was drawn to the West.

Three evenly spaced vertical lines crossed through three evenly spaced horizontal lines, with both sets of lines crossing through three evenly spaced concentric circles. The triple cross-upon-circle motif seemed to depict something between a snowflake and a spider's web.

"It is a symbol of Fate," Hawk informed. "That charm belongs to my Brother, but he doesn't wear it and I don't need to hold onto it any longer." The Indian revealed more about himself than he had in a very long time. His comfort around Jacobi was unusual, as he mostly shunned the company of white strangers. "You'll learn and decide what it means to you eventually. Thus is Fate."

There's that phrase again: thus is Fate.

"But, will your brother...miss this?"

The Indian didn't answer that question.

"Just as the eagle that beats its wings to soar affects which winds we breathe," Hawk said, "your Fate is already being woven into the lives of others."

A sharp gunshot rang out in the distance, echoing as black birds flew from trees, bringing the possibility of any more answers for Jacobi to an end.

More shots were fired.

Hawk moved swiftly.

Jacobi was alarmed, but relieved that these were real gunshots that someone else could hear.

The discharge of gunfire continued to exchange as the sounds of galloping horses and wagon wheels approached directly toward the camp.

Bursting through the brush into the campsite, an open-topped wagon drawn by two horses veered to miss the fire, but the vehicle drifted and smashed the hanging pot's hot contents over. The driver, a grey-bearded man dressed in the rough fur and leather trappings of a frontier survivalist, finally brought the horses to a wrenching halt.

"Fugging Renegades on my tail!" He began reloading his rifle. "Where's Royce?"

Hawk quickly grabbed a bow from within a cow hide; the same antler bow Jacobi had seen in his visions while being cocooned by the giant spider. The Indian tossed him a revolver, which he fumbled to catch.

Three men in dishevelled grey military coats galloped in upon horses, firing their own revolvers. Hawk had already drawn and loosed an arrow into the intruder on the left, the greycoat falling to the earth with his horse fleeing the area.

"Shoot, Jacobi!" Hawk urged as he reached for another arrow. "They will not offer you the same mercy of hesitation that you offer them."

"The coats," the bearded man shouted, still reloading, "shoot the greycoats! Shoot the Renegades!"

With sheer panic, Jacobi held the gun toward the second man, his eyes shut tight, squeezing the trigger as many times as he could, the exploding sounds and recoil forcing him to stumble back.

Of the five bullets Jacobi fired, one found its mark in the rider's chest. As his target hit the ground, Hawk finished the greycoat by stabbing him in the chest with a knife crafted of bone.

Jacobi fell to the ground, a ringing inside his head, rattled by his first use of a gun and the mortal truth that he had just contributed to killing a man.

The third greycoat was shot in the back three times, the grip on his weapon released, his attacker bursting from the trees after him.

Hawk lowered his next arrow.

On a horse that was the colour of fire, a man with wild snow-white hair had emptied his revolver's chamber into his target.

"About time, Royce," the grey-bearded trapper shook his head at the latest entrant, still loading. "Where'd you get to?"

"Circling back behind that one," Royce motioned to the third greycoat that hadn't even fallen from his horse yet, "so I could save your miserable hide, Miller." He tilted his head. "You can thank me later."

Jacobi's world spun a little, the new arrivals—and departures—swirling around his head to the ringing. As the third greycoat eventually fell and his horse fled, his killer was at Jacobi's side.

Royce took the bowler hat from atop his ragged white hair and extended it upside-down into the dizzy-looking stranger's lap. "If you need to spew, greenhorn, spew into this." Raising a pale eyebrow, he added, "But if you do manage to yack into my hat, I'll kill ya."

He looked from Jacobi to Hawk and Miller, thumb indicating to where the wagon had entered. "I rendered another bunch of these fuggers dead, back there, but there's more of these Renegade scum coming.

Royce pulled a revolver that was tucked in his belt and squeezed it into Jacobi's right hand. "Pull that hammer back, aim that end into the bad guy, pull the trigger. Repeat. Got it? You're up again, greenhorn, we're not out of this yet."

CHAPTER

SIX

More of the raucous grey-coated Renegades spilled into the wooded area in their own single-horse wagon. One driver and five passengers brandishing rifles and revolvers. Among the passengers was one sporting an eyepatch, commanding them.

"The war's over, Fuggedds!" Royce called to them, raising the barrels of two large revolvers beside his face while he found a tree trunk for cover. "Or did they forget to tell you?"

"The War never ended," the eye-patched one answered. "All your supplies are hereby forfeit to the Renegades, as are your lives upon refusal to enlist in the Movement."

A bullet found one of the Renegades that had just reached ground from the wagon, Miller's rifle answering with him. "Yep, we heard it from the first lot that tried to conscript us. They didn't much like our response neither."

"Redskin!" another Renegade pointed.

The greycoats focused their gunfire upon Hawk, as though he was suddenly the greatest threat under the woodland canopy of the campsite.

The Indian had loosed an unsuccessful arrow because he had to dive for cover to escape becoming riddled with holes.

"Racist Busduds." Royce reached a barrel toward them, firing.

"Renegades don't want no prairie ni—"

Royce had quickly exchanged one of his guns for the camp's toppled coffee pot, throwing the hot vessel by the handle at the greycoat before he could finish his slur. He used the distraction to put a bullet from his other gun into the Renegade's head. "Yeah, but he'd be the best of you!"

A greycoat came for Jacobi as the young man fumbled with the hammer of the spare revolver Royce had thrust upon him.

The gun Hawk had given him first didn't need the hammer pulled back. You just pulled the trigger and the hammer obeyed. Which was lucky for him as he didn't know what he was doing around these weapons. His Boston life had been so...*civilised*. The need to learn firearms hadn't arisen. But a few minutes in the Wild West and Jacobi was in over his head with gun troubles.

His anxiousness was reaching a peak as he somehow had the hammer of Royce's weapon stuck between cocked and not.

Miller shot the oncoming greycoat when Jacobi finally managed to hear the satisfying click of a fully cocked hammer.

Hawk returned swiftly from his cover, an axe being swung overhead but with no foe in front of him.

But he wasn't swinging it—and it was no ordinary axe—it was decorated with coloured strapping, beads and feathers. It was a tomahawk. Just like Jacobi had read in cheap novels with gaudy illustrations.

The tomahawk was thrown with a precise overarm motion, the axe rotating one full cycle, the distinctive weapon striking with its sharp edge into the Renegade's chest.

Before the man had a chance to fall upon the axe, Hawk had moved faster than Jacobi thought could be possible. The Indian had closed distance and retrieved his weapon, leapt upon the greycoats' wagon to then make a few steps at an angle and spring toward another foe.

The next Renegade received the tomahawk in the side of his skull before he could fathom what was going on. As a woodcutter fells a tree, Hawk had felled the man.

Rusty never hid during the whole encounter, despite Royce trying to send him away a few times. The loyal red dog ran interference, barking and growling here and there, wreaking havoc with the aim of the Renegades.

The last one, the one with the eyepatch, was upon Miller. "You carry yourself like a Serviceman. Which side are you on?"

"Fugginell, the War's over!" Stepping back to avoid the oncoming Renegade wasn't enough. "But you guys just won't hear it, will you?"

The graycoat knocked Miller's rifle aside with his own. The enemy muscled in closer until he had the barrel of his own weapon stabbing under Miller's bearded chin.

Dropping his rifle and raising his hands to surrender, Miller knew his life was over.

With a wry grin, the Renegade breathed an audible delight, "Well I'm here to tell you the War never ended."

Before the Renegade could finish pulling his trigger, his remaining eye was shot out from behind, his lifeless body hitting the camp floor.

After a second or two of shock, a blood-spattered Miller gathered himself up and answered the dead man. "And I'm still standing here to tell you again...the War's fugging over."

Looking around, Miller realised that the Renegades were all defeated and that the reverse-eyeball-shot had come from a very pale young stranger with a familiar bowler hat in his lap. "Am I..." A smoking revolver hung by its trigger guard from a limp finger. He realised that the young man had just saved his life. "Am I...glad..."

Royce emerged from some trees with a chuckle. "I think what the old man is trying to say, is that he's glad you bullseyed that Renegade."

"Lucky..." Miller shook his head.

"I know," Royce added. "What are the chances of this greenhorn taking out that diggedd's good eyeball...and from behind? I mean, come on—from behind?"

"I mean...lucky for me, kid. Am I glad that you came along."

Miller's age was difficult to discern as he continued to gather himself. His skin was creased and weathered above the beard, and he moved slower than Royce and especially Hawk. The Renegade had said something about the way he carried himself. *A Serviceman*. A soldier, perhaps? He stroked the wagon's two horses, calming them, thanking them for being so brave. He looked at the hole in his last attacker's remaining eye, then to Jacobi.

"Judging by the colour of our stranger's face, I guess that could have been me with the bullet."

Jacobi dropped the revolver, a burnt smell filling his nostrils. His hands shook, a painful tingle shooting from his fingers up each arm. He wasn't sure what was happening, if it was from the gun's recoil, or grasping the fact that this time he was singularly responsible for taking a man's life.

He hadn't thrown up into Royce's hat, so at least he had that in his favour.

"And howdy, Hawk," Miller greeted, recovering himself as though a gunfight was an everyday occurrence. He looked at the ruined campfire and up-righted the hurled pot, his face screwing up with shame. "Well, I guess I missed Hawk's coffee?"

"A pity, My Friend." Hawk tapped his fist to his chest. "Because our new *Friend* says it was *amazing*."

"Fancy throwing the pot, Royce." Miller breathed frustration, head dipped, face shaking from side to side.

"Hey," Royce argued, picking up spent cartridge casings from the woodland floor, "that pot had already been tipped over before I arrived. I blame your bad driving."

"I blame the horses..." Miller jested.

"Hah!" Royce pulled a twig from his jungle of snow-white hair. "Those horses can probably drive a wagon better without you."

Ignoring Royce, Miller asked with a casual calm, "And who is our new...Friend?"

Miller noticed the pendant hanging from the distressed stranger's chest, as had Royce.

"This is Jacobi Nicholson," Hawk answered. "I'm hoping you can take him with you on the next run and show him how things are done in the West?"

"A stranger to the West, eh?" Miller said.

Royce made an observation as he put spent casings into his pocket. "Greenhorn, you look like tragedy on legs. But I'd say you've just studied at the best school in the West. And I don't just mean Hawk here, I mean getting into a scrap with those Renegades."

Miller looked at the sorry young man that had obviously been chewed up and spat out by the Wild West. "We'll have to teach you how to shoot."

"More often," Royce smirked.

"And I hope those injuries won't stop you from being able to work. Everybody pulls their weight around here. We have deliveries to make."

LUKE TRACEY

"The first lesson, "Royce added, "should probably be how to dispose of dead bandits. You don't want the Law finding them or worse...have them *come back*."

Before Jacobi could ask what that last part actually meant, Miller extended a gloved hand. "Howdy, the name's *Miller*."

Royce did the same. "Name's Falco, Royce Falco. You may have seen my mug on wanted posters. Just ignore those...they're all lies...well...mostly..."

Royce had been studying Jacobi. Everything from his slashed attire, wounds, uneasiness with weapons and combat, all the way to the specific pendant that adorned his neck. That pendant, in particular, being worn by the greenhorn, begged answers.

Jacobi accepted Miller's hand, being pulled up to his feet, shaking it after. "P-pleased to meet you, Mister Miller, is it?. And you too, Mister Falco. Um, well, I'm Jacobi Nicholson, of Bost....well, I'm from wherever here is now."

"Real proper, isn't he? Shell-shocked, but still proper." Miller looked to Hawk and back, smiling, as Royce took over the hand shake with the young man. "Well, son, I don't know where you want to be, but you're in the frontiers of the Wild West. *Takoda Territory.* Where the *Horse Nation* rides. Just west of the mighty *Missouri* River and very west of the mighty *Mississippi* River. The long bits of water that together we like to call the *Raging Rubicon River.*"

"Also," Hawk added, "please take him to see Charles Lafayette."

"Really?" Miller dropped his smile, annoyance crossing his face.

Royce emitted a curious tone, crossing his arms, focusing again on the pendant, interest spreading farther across his face.

Despite the sudden shift in greeting, Jacobi's eyes lit up with recognition of the mysterious card playing magician's name. But with Miller's obvious dissatisfaction over Charles Lafayette's mention, he wondered whether it was worth bringing it up.

Royce enquired. "It sounds like you've hatched another plan, which also sounds like you're not coming. So where are you going, Hawk?"

"To continue tracking Twyla Matthias."

And there's that name again, too, Jacobi thought.

Hawk didn't let anyone respond, interrupting the exchange with a chirping whistle that sounded like a bird. The horse that had dragged Jacobi's mortally wounded body by travois to the campsite trotted into the area, responding with a whinny to the Indian's whistled call.

As Jacobi retrieved the revolver given to him from the ground, he observed unusual horizontal dark stripes encircling the legs in the horse's golden-tan coat. The West held many new things to observe, and the young man had seen so much in so few days.

"The steamer she is on is headed to Rosewood. Then she'll head overland to Sundown before going on to Boom Town." Hawk loaded his saddle with packed bags onto the horse, including tomahawks and plenty of arrows for his antler bow. "If the situation is right between Rosewood and Sundown, I'm finally going to end this whole thing."

"Let me come," Royce tried, but was ignored. "You don't want to run into any of her cronies alone."

"That does worry me some." Miller's frown lines creased with concern, seeing the finality in Hawk's speech. "But just tell me this then. Why the fugg do we need to visit that dandy, Chuck Lafayette?"

"Because," Hawk replied as he guided his horse from the camp, Rusty following, his answer leaving Miller speechless and Royce more curious.

"I believe that Jacobi Nicholson does not realise that he already rides the Thunder Road. Not only have the Ghost Riders appeared to him near death, but he has the talent to spin Wyrd..."

PART III

SPINNING WYRD

CHAPTER

SEVEN

"The grey one on your left, he's *Sarge*," Miller explained, "and the dark brown one on your right, she's *Maple Stirrup*."

Jacobi laughed. "Maple *Stirrup*, really?"

"Fugg yeah, kid. Won her from a Canadian. Funny guy. Lousy card player."

When Royce rode ahead of their wagon, Miller added, "And that one there, he's Firefly, which you can see obviously comes from his fiery coat, and not-so-much from the colour of his rider's hair."

Royce called back over his shoulder, ignoring Miller's quip, "And he can fly like the wind!"

Jacobi smiled. "Yeah, I've never seen hair so unlike fire in my life."

Miller gave a gentle frown. "Your head still feeling cracked, son? What're you talking about? Royce is as ginger as a sunset."

His mouth opened, but no words came out of Jacobi.

"What?" Miller's eyes thinned.

"His hair is clearly as white as snow..."

"You are cracked..." Miller chuckled. "He didn't get any of the dark hair from his brother's side of the family."

Jacobi still looked as though he didn't know what was going on.

Miller filled him in. "Royce is Hawk's half-brother. German and Takoda Indian parents. It's why he looks like a dandy. Some say his face is pretty, but I usually just want to punch it." Miller laughed.

Jacobi touched the pendant around his neck. "Royce is Hawk's brother..."

"Yeah, that's what I said. And I see your wearing Hawk's old necklace."

"He gave it to me. Said it was his brother's and that he wouldn't need it."

"Did he? Yeah, Royce used to wear that, he threw it away, then Hawk picked it up."

"Why do you call him, Hawk?"

"That's a stupid question, kid. Because it's his name."

"What about, *Shev*?"

Miller slowed the horses. "How the fugg do you know that name?"

"He told me." Jacobi tried not to be alarmed.

The wagon halted.

"He doesn't tell nobody that. I mean nobody. There's a lot of history. He doesn't trust us white folk, and he's got every reason not to. I'm lucky he trusts me at all."

"He said it is his name to friends," Jacobi explained, wondering if he should ever repeat the name again.

Miller started the wagon, the horses whinnying.

"So...you fall overboard. Hawk rescues you from all sorts of nasties. You talk a bit and he tells you his *sacred* name."

"I guess that's the simple version."

"And you think Royce has white hair."

Jacobi agreed. "Uh-huh."

Miller's eyes opened wide. "You really are fugging cracked in the head. Or, Hawk sees something in you that we can't. He's like that.

Royce is a bit like that too…or was. They drive me nuts. The pair of them. But Hawk, he's an old sort of Indian wizard."

"A wizard? Like in books and myths?"

"Well, you know, medicine man and all that sort of thing. Like an Indian version of Chuck Lafayette."

"So he's a magician too?"

"No," Miller didn't have the right words. "Royce is a bit like Chuck, but just a bit. Hawk is more like some kind of nature wizard."

"A shaman?"

"Yeah, kid," the veteran nodded. "That's it. A shaman. He's all about the weather and omens and trees and animals and shid. The way it seems he was telling you everything, he probably would have told you more if he hadn't taken off suddenly on his horse."

"That horse, Hawk had a very interesting horse."

"He calls that one, *Strider*. Holds some significance to him."

"It had striped legs. I've never seen stripes on a horse's legs before."

"He's sired from old horse blood. Very old blood."

Miller suddenly frowned. "Anyways, stop changing the subject with all these questions. You're gonna have heaps more after we get to Chuck. What was I harping on about before you sidetracked me?"

"My name," Jacobi answered.

"Yeah, that's right. As I was saying. Your name's too difficult to keep saying out loud. You could get shot in town just for having a name like *Jacobi*. Tell you what. We gotta come up with a new name for you."

"I told Hawk that some people call me, *Jack*."

"I was just thinking of Jack. Jack is better. Jack's bullet-proof—well, almost. I'm calling you *Jack*. If you had been a soldier, it wouldn't be a problem because I'd be calling you Nicholson. And that's why everybody calls me Miller. Everyone. Including you, son. But you ain't been in the Service. I have."

"So that bandit was right about you?" Jacobi asked.

"He was." Miller sighed. "Soldiers, especially past soldiers, can usually recognise each other. At first, I was conscripted into the war for the South. Later on, I met Sarge here."

"The Confederacy?"

"Yep. The fugging Confederates." Miller shook his head. "I didn't like it. But that was where I lived. And I had to wear the same grey coat as those Renegades."

Jacobi realised that he had Miller leaving his name alone and answering questions again. "Who are they...or were they...and why do you call them Renegades?"

"*They* call themselves Renegades." Miller thought how best to describe them. "They're an outlaw militia. Worse, they're bandits, thieves and robbers. And they don't reckon that they lost the war. To them, the war never ended. To the Renegades, the war still goes on, they're still fighting for their *way of life* while the rest of the South reconstructs."

"What could they possibly want?"

"They didn't like change. They wanted things the same. The worst of it is that they still want people that look like Chuck Lafayette clapped in irons."

"Slavery...?"

Miller nodded an affirmation with a bowed head. "The war never did reach you in Boston, did it, kid?"

"No," Jacobi answered. "Boston did a lot to get it going, though, and sent soldiers."

"Awful. The whole damned thing. But it freed a lot of good folk."

As the horse-drawn wagon rolled along the dirt road closer toward the settlement of Mudflats, the smoke from chimneys could be seen rising over the wet brown earth.

"Anyway, as I was saying before when I first got tripped up on your name, *Jack*, I'm telling you: I was with Chuck Lafayette that night. He even made me go through a stupid song and dance to make him appear. There's no way he was on your boat during the days you say."

"Song and dance?" Jacobi wondered what that meant and didn't know what more to say. "I promise you; a man of the exact same name and description was seated at the same poker table on the *River Grace*..."

Miller spat his trail gum, almost with disgust.

"Fugging Chuck. And don't be telling Royce I just spat that out. The man hates spoiling nature, even if this trodden road already spoiled it before my gum did."

That reminded Jacobi of seeing Royce picking up the spent bullet casings earlier.

"I do actually believe you," Miller looked to Jacobi. "But trust me, if you get to know Chuck, you'll be banging your head against a fugging brick wall in no time with all the tricks and nonsense he pulls."

As Miller handled the reins, Jacobi realised there was a third on board.

It had been raining before their wagon reached the area. Miller had even mentioned, "Lucky we didn't need the cover on the wagon," but the clouds had since parted.

The red dog stood on hind legs amongst the crafted goods, front paws holding onto the edge of the wagon bed. He let the new morning sun warm his fur and the breeze flow through his face and tongue.

"How long has Rusty been with us?"

Miller looked back to the stowaway, watching the dog's happy tongue. "Not long. Happens all the time. He probably came back after us when he realised that he couldn't keep up with Hawk...or that Hawk didn't want him tagging along."

"Hawk would leave his dog behind?"

"No, never." Miller put his eyes back on the damp trail. "Rusty doesn't really have a master. Although, Royce'd say it's him. Rusty has friends; he's an equal. He's part of the team...our group. He comes and goes as he pleases, but he rarely leaves unless there's a problem. He's the messenger between friends that aren't always together, that keep on moving from place to place."

"He's like a telegram."

"*Like a telegram*...I like that, kid."

"Does he always find one of you?"

"Every time, Jack." Miller nodded with happy memories crossing his face. "He can go from settlement to settlement. Hunt to feed and water himself. Carry mail. Pull part of a camp. And still find his way back to any of us." He turned to Jacobi. "He can even help nurse a wayward greenhorn back to health."

"What is a greenhorn?" Jacobi asked.

The husky broke the conversation with a bark, leaping out of the wagon to run on ahead.

Three ravens fled into the air above where Rusty ran as Miller explained, "That means we're here."

CHAPTER

EIGHT

The logging town of Rosewood received trade boats and larger river ships on the west side of the Rubicon. The smell of fresh cut lumber was adrift in what would soon become the night air. No matter the time of day, there was always the scent of western redcedar flowing through the streets. And, if the wind blew westerly just right from the river, there could also be an aromatic hint of fresh water on that same breeze.

Hawk was well hidden. His skill for remaining undetected was acquired through years of evading soldiers that hunted his people, among the many other forms of pursuer he'd encountered in his life. Stealth came easy to him, especially when he was able to use natural brush and wooded areas.

Rosewood was a town proudly built from its distant trees, its architecture a sight of beautiful carpentry. Western motifs of animals, wagons and river culture blended together—statuesque carvings of redcedar. Log cabins were rare, as almost every chance was taken to craft the wood like an artform. Balustrades, architraves and decorative gables appeared as though they were the work of ancient sculptors rather than modern carpenters. The majority of the immediate trees remained as part of Rosewood's aesthetic character, giant sentinels that towered over the town. It was this generous sympathy toward allowing nature to survive that provided an abundance of places for Hawk to hide.

During the last hours of daylight, he had carefully led his horse through Rosewood. Hawk used the brim of his hat, the collar of his shirt, and some riding gloves, to best hide his heritage from ignorant folk that wouldn't want to see their accustomed peace broken by a savage entering their pretty town.

LUKE TRACEY

Listening to townsfolk was good for catching local gossip about anyone coming or going, but Rosewood was quiet on this day. The most scandalous event so far had been that a brazen infant, wooden toy sword in hand ready to deliver retribution, had chased their thieving sibling down a road in response to their wooden toy horse being stolen.

He had passed with Strider by a seedy saloon that had fresh water in a trough at the front for hitched horses. The sign above, a bold timber relief carving, named the saloon:

TIMBERLANDS

He had passed a building with some carefree ladies leaning out the windows. That place's hung sign read:

MORNING WOOD

And the...

UNDERTAKER

...well, there was no clever name and no pine boxes there, but you can be sure that there were plenty of redcedar coffins.

They certainly were all about their wood here, Hawk thought, obsessed.

After feeding the horse their last apple and letting him drink, Hawk cupped Strider's long head against his own and said, "No matter what happens, I want you to know, that in all of the time we have shared, you have been a faithful companion."

Some patrons heading into the saloon—both already drunk before arriving—overheard the exchange.

"What'd that hobo say?" one of them asked.

"I dunno," the other answered. "Something about an *onion*..."

After scouting a few locations, Hawk had found the perfect hiding spot where he and Strider could unload their trappings to prepare and remain undetected. It had a good vantage of the water vessels coming and going, looking over the length of Rosewood's dock.

After leaving Royce and Miller with the death-defying survivor, Jacobi, Hawk had caught up alongside the River Grace along the water's edge and ridden well ahead of the steamer. Strider's speed never failed. This time there weren't any incidents with overboard passengers to be dealt with. The last to fall, at least, had confirmed Twyla Matthias was disembarking at Rosewood, but was able to add that she was heading next to Sundown before moving on to Boom Town. Knowing a mapped journey like that could prove useful. This had given ample time to scout the best locations to spy from and see the potential places that she may visit while in Rosewood.

Meeting with Jacobi had been fortuitous. That much was certain. It seemed Fate landed the young man in their care and his presence had already saved a life and affected a major decision. Sending him to meet with Charles Lafayette should shed some light on whether Jacobi was some sort of mystic prodigy in the scions of Fate or just the tragic recipient of a streak of seriously bad luck.

And thinking of Charles Lafayette; Jacobi had said that he was onboard the *River Grace*. Much to the incredulity of Miller. And there should be another young man by the name of Francis that could be in some trouble with the Gold Baroness.

As the paddle steamer came into view, Hawk knew he needed to keep a discerning watch over those disembarking. Waiting for the ship had been the easy part. Getting to Twyla Matthias was going to be the hard part.

CHAPTER

NINE

Miller entered a crossroads of soaked earth at the outskirts of Mudflats. The roads didn't lead to anything special, except for the one that passed on ahead through Mudflats.

He slowed their open-top cart wagon alongside an enclosed caravan wagon that was so large Jacobi thought it was practically a small house on wheels. It wasn't what he'd call a *normal* wagon, and its wheels weren't *normal* wagon wheels either; they were solid metal.

Royce was leaning upon the huge wagon. He spun a playing card in his hand: the Two of Clubs.

THUNDER ROAD

"What's a greenhorn, you ask?" Royce grinned. "You, Jacobi Nicholson, of Boston, Massachusetts, you're a greenhorn."

"That doesn't really answer my question."

Royce helped the wounded greenhorn climb down from the wagon's seat, Miller handing him the crutch Hawk had crafted. Despite the wagon's vibrations, the journey had made Jacobi almost forget his ailments.

Almost.

Jacobi had seen some ostentatious displays while travelling East to West that were used to sell the strangest curios. But this massive black wagon, a caravan, with gold decorations was signed with matching gilded lettering that read like the front of a cheap newspaper advertisement.

The One & Only
CHARLES LAFAYETTE
Illusionist. Magician. Perceptivist.
Master of Cosmology,
Esoterica, Fortuna,
Portentia and Mysticism.
Purveyor of the Wyrd & Wonderful.

Jacobi mouthed the words, *Charles Lafayette*, forming the name that seemed to follow him wherever he went—said to even do the impossible by being in two places at once!

Miller explained to Jacobi, "Thank fugg for that. We didn't have to do a song and dance to make him appear..."

"I've already taken care of that," Royce explained.

Jacobi still didn't understand what any of that meant and realised that there were three ravens perched on the black caravan above Royce's head.

He was sure they weren't there before.

And he was sure three blackbirds had already flown off as they approached this area.

The apparently not-white-haired man then motioned toward the caravan. "And I know what you're thinking, greenhorn: looks like some kind of hobo snake oil salesman's beat-up shop on wheels."

Jacobi nodded yes, it did.

It did indeed.

Yet those wheels weren't right.

"But this is the real deal, kid." Royce flipped his card into his other hand, and it was suddenly the Ace of Skulls.

No doubt. It was the Ace of Skulls.

It would have been unfamiliar if Jacobi had not seen the strange suit before in a quick flash aboard the *River Grace*.

As clear as day. The Two of Clubs had instantly become the Ace of Skulls! And Royce followed the spectacle by flipping the card around his knuckles until it vanished from existence as though it was nothing out of the ordinary, a flourish of shifting fingers finishing the trick.

And suddenly the ravens were gone. There were no black wings spread in the sky, and no sound of such things. The birds were just not present any longer.

There were no horses to be seen and no sign that anyone lived adjacent: just this unattended caravan with glittering adornments on the side of the crossroad.

Rusty rushed up the few stairs at the back of the caravan and quickly disappeared inside through a hanging door that was just the right size for him, leaving it swinging within the bottom of an average-sized door.

Within seconds, something fell over inside the caravan—possibly breaking—and a black cat bolted out of the little door. It was soon chased by the red dog that had immediately gone looking for it.

"It is perfectly all right." A familiar voice opened the door, the occupant looking immediately to Jacobi. "These wonderful creatures are well acquainted."

Jacobi almost fell from his crutch. It was indeed the magician from the *River Grace*. There could be no mistake.

"Same man?" Miller asked.

"The very same," Jacobi confirmed.

The veteran shook his head with an irritated want to disbelieve.

"Do not be frightened," the magician spoke, "unless you were followed by some Terrorgators and their Trikuhl masters."

The magician paused for dramatic effect.

Jacobi was stunned. Not from the particular annunciation of the spider-monster's name or the fact that it was dropped in simple conversation, but stunned by the apparent number of the creatures. "*Trikuhl...masters*...meaning there's more than one of those things?"

"Always a possibility—their web is vast. But a sharp lad such as yourself in the company of these two rapscallions wouldn't be followed by a Trikuhl. Would you?"

"Uh," Jacobi's eyes searched the area with worry. He was still becoming accustomed to the fact that what he had witnessed at the river could be real...no, was real...it was real...and not some near-death delusion. "No...could we have been?"

The caravan's occupant didn't answer as he glided down the small set of stairs, a swiftness of step as a cape flowed behind the same ensemble he had worn on the *River Grace*. He smirked at the wounded Jacobi's mortal concern. "Excellent. It would have been most inconvenient if such monstrosities had interrupted this fortunate meeting that Fate has provided."

The man's midnight blue suit and wide-brimmed hat were as flamboyant as some of the gold lettering he pointed to. "These are freshly signed, Miller. What do you think?"

"What do I think?" Miller thumbed to himself. "Forget the letters." He pointed to the steel wheels. "What's with the train wheels on your wagon?"

"They're not *train* wheels unless they are on a locomotive."

"They are so train wheels!" Miller pointed at a crescent shape that was on the end of the metal spokes at the edge of each wheel. "They clearly have balancing weights."

With a cocky eyebrow, Lafayette explained, "Ordinary wagon wheels are just that; they are ordinary! These wheels have the distinction of being *extra*-ordinary."

"Yeah? Well a flat wagon wheel won't dig into the ground like the flanges of these wheels will. Without train tracks, you're bogged."

Jacobi covered his mouth with the back of his hand to stifle an amused grin, seeing Royce also smirking at the argument.

"Please cast the wheels from your mind, my confounded friend. We will speak of them at a later date." Lafayette drew the attention back to the lettering. "What do you think about the fresh lettering?"

Miller sighed. "You've changed some words." The veteran pointed at painted letters that were fresher than others.

"Indeed!" The magician looked to Jacobi. "Our Miller still possesses a youthful cunning that belies his true age."

Royce piped up. "So where's Kamiko?"

"I should explain," Lafayette began, but continued to answer toward Jacobi. "You see, M'Laddo, *Occultist* and *Sorcerer* were not having the effect in civilised La Grande that I had hoped for. My dear assistant, Miss Kamiko Watanabe. We had a disagreement on some matters of Fate, which resulted in her...resignation. And I was most unceremoniously...asked...to leave town."

"Ran out of town again, more like it." Miller crossed his arms, choking laughter in his throat.

Lafayette admitted, "Well, it was an event, to be sure, but I wouldn't go so far as to call it an *attempted lynching*. At the very least, not this time."

"So Kamiko's gone now?" Royce was disappointed, following his question with a little kick of the dirt.

Jacobi noticed that the white-haired man didn't have spurs on his boots as Miller did.

The veteran shook his head. "So how many times is that now, Chuck? Just don't get into trouble here in Mudflats and lose us a good source of trade. They're decent people with trustworthy coin. Or, lose the chance to have a chat with Jack here."

"Dear Alfred,"—that was the first time Jacobi heard Miller's given name—"you know it pains me so when you reduce my appellation to such a simple sobriquet as *Chuck*, as though you're some common barroom ruffian. Despite the slight toward me, I will certainly converse with young...*Jacobi Nicholson*. Is it not? For that was your name when we met above the water level on the *River Grace*. Not this, *Jack*, which is sure to be a shorthand invention of our veteran associate, Alfred Miller."

"I guess," Jacobi shrugged, "it's changing."

Royce added, "Also answers to greenhorn," with a wink.

The magician tipped the wide brim of his dark hat toward Jacobi, acknowledging that they had met without being asked.

"Where are my manners? I'm positively aghast with embarrassment." He extended a white-gloved hand to Jacobi. "As you know, I am Charles Lafayette, Purveyor of the Wyrd and Wonderful. But, if it suits you, I will gladly accept...*Magician*."

Jacobi bit his lip, softly, "I thought you realised that we've already met."

"Of course, M'Laddo." Charles Lafayette twizzled his dark moustache. "But never stop a magician when he takes a chance to practice his performance."

Miller rolled his eyes. "Apparently you met Jack on a steamboat when you and I were actually together last."

"Indeed," the magician answered.

Miller grunted. "You're not going to explain how you were in two places at once, are you?"

"But, Alfred, was I?"

"Fuggsake." Miller looked at Jacobi. "This is what Chuck does. Get used to it." He grunted again. "Hawk sent me with Jack to...anyway, Jack saw some things you'd know about."

Royce delivered a smile so wide his teeth shined. "What Miller's also trying to say is that Hawk said the greenhorn can spin Wyrd."

Charles raised an arm to the entryway of his caravan. "Well...*thus is Fate.*"

There's that phrase again.

"Come, M'Laddo, let me assist you to ascend this stairwell. I'm sure you have many-a-question."

Miller headed back to the wagon of crafted goods. "Hawk has gone tracking Twyla Matthias again." He looked at Lafayette with great sincerity. "Apparently to finally end it. I kinda believe him this time. Anyway, I'll leave you two to get to know each other while Royce and I go into Mudflats to trade this load."

Climbing back on board the wagon, Miller took the reins, starting the horses on their way. "And, Chuck? Be kind to the kid, eh?"

Lafayette acknowledged with a tip of his hat's wide brim. "There are paths aplenty ahead of us all. It is best that we each tread carefully for good fortune, but with a renewal of determined purpose."

"Hey, Greenhorn." Royce tapped his spurless boot against Firefly to follow the wagon. "When you're in there with the magician: forget what you know, or think you know." He waved a parting. "Say goodbye to your notions of the Wild West. Things are about to get a whole lot stranger. Welcome now, to the Wyrd West..."

CHAPTER

TEN

When the steamboat began to sidle with the dock, he dropped the hat from his head and the clothes from his shoulders. With an opposite heel he forced his boots from the other in turn, baring his feet.

Hawk withdrew small bladders of paint from Strider's saddlebags. He slid a pointed finger across his face with red and some black. Taking white, he dotted his chest and shoulders. Taking the red again, he scrawled with simple lines and circles a bird with its head and wings spread from a centre that resembled what was now Jacobi's pendant.

From a deep recess of Strider's saddlebags, he retrieved something wrapped in a protective blanket. The covering was a woven Takoda pattern featuring buffalo drinking at a creek. He took the weapon out, holding it aloft. Below an iron head, beads were affixed to the shaft and the feather of a bird of prey hung from it. The poll opposite the axe blade was shaped like a tiny bowl. Some would call it an Indian throwing axe, others a Takoda tomahawk. To Hawk, this weapon was more than that, and at that point in time it was the weapon he felt most comfortable closing quarters with.

And his most skilled with.

Orders were called as the *River Grace* pounded against the lamp-lit dock. The redcedar wood wrenched in powerful defiance of the vessel under the red light of a sun that hadn't yet given way to night. Ropes were thrown by uniformed boat crew, ramps were levelled, carts were hustled. Luggage was carted from the boat to an empty area of the dock where it would wait to be claimed.

A handful of soldiers approached, loitering around the dock. Hawk hadn't seen their blue uniforms in town when he was performing what Miller would call *recon*.

This was unexpected.

And unwelcome.

Very unwelcome.

"Not good," he said to his horse.

But it was not uncommon. Twyla Matthias was well-connected and able to line the pockets of the right people. She shared many interests and goals as that of the growing United States and some of its more amoral officials—those of the clandestine Sicarius Assembly—which was to exert a stronger influence farther westward.

Manifest Destiny, some called it.

With the soldiers, but standing as though unwelcome among their number, was a meek individual. He wore goggles fogged with grease and cradled a device as though he were mimicking the way that the military men around him held their rifles. His attire consisted of a thick shirt and trousers with a heavy apron and long bulky protective gloves. On top of his equally greasy hair was a leather cap you'd expect to see someone working in a mine wearing. The hat was complete with a small, bizarre dish on the front that glowed in the night. The device in his hands was some form of oversized weapon, no doubt, perhaps an advanced rifle. The contraption blinked with a couple of coloured lights and hissed with escaping vapour.

Hawk didn't even need to see behind the goggles to know who this man was. "Why are you here? Victor Quartus Falco."

Fourth of eight Falco brothers.

A crazy scientist: a *gizmologist*.

"Shid." Hawk muttered to Strider. "Having a Falco family member present that isn't Royce changes things." Hawk was going to need to reassess the situation. "I can't strike while a Falco is there."

The luggage of Twyla Matthias was on the dock of Rosewood well before she was. When she walked down the ramp, there were a few admiring exhales, just the reaction she always tried to elicit. She wore the latest dress from Paris—so she was informed—turquoise and white with matching bonnet adorned with large flowers and feathered plumes. The final unusual flourish that separated her from others was a gunbelt housing a revolver and a sword sheathed in a metal scabbard.

It was a sabre.

A military sabre, to be precise. No doubt gifted from one of her associates. Probably Captain Phileas Cordell.

Hawk noticed something flicker about Twyla, like an eclipse of moths around a flame. But there were no moths, the few that were gathering in the oncoming dusk danced around the lamps of the dock. The flicker moved, like a fleeting shadow, but as Hawk tried to focus upon it...the vague phenomenon slipped away like the memory of a dream being woken from.

Hawk wondered, was the Trikuhl here?

"Ma'am," one of the soldiers greeted. "I trust your voyage was comfortable."

"Comfortable, yes," she answered, "but it was certainly not uneventful."

"Captain Cordell sends his regards. We are to provide protection to your stage on your journey to Sundown. We are to leave your company to rejoin Captain Cordell upon your safe delivery."

"Trouble, soldier?"

"The Indian problem has escalated."

"That's all fine by me, soldier." She mock saluted the young man. "I'll hire some thugs in

Sundown. That place is full of dullards with muscles and no brains."

"Certainly."

"Also, there's a young man on board that owes me. Francis Geddes. He's signed a contract to work his debt off in Boom Town. See that he is transported directly there."

"Certainly, Ma'am." The soldier waved some of his men to follow him onto the *River Grace*.

"And how about you, Vick?" She raised her eyebrows to the Falco inventor. "Always a man of many words."

"Ah," Victor was always awkward, "not as such, just nothing interesting to add. Cordell had me tag along to help as I needed to meet a contact in Sundown about some spare parts."

"I assume, for your gun?"

"My *lightning accelerator*, Ma'am." A small amount of pride crept across Victor's face. "I'm on the verge of another electrifying breakthrough."

"Aren't you always."

Victor didn't know if he was supposed to be insulted or not.

Hawk studied the dock. The steamboat security and staff. The soldiers. Victor Falco. And the target herself, Twyla Matthias.

"Shid," Hawk cussed under his breath again. "We have to leave."

He slipped his hat, shirt and boots back on while murmuring a chant, asking the trees to guide him unseen under cover of darkness.

He led his horse toward some drunks that were stumbling away from the middle of town. Hawk would have normally avoided them, but their predictable behaviour could be useful for blending into the Rosewood night.

"We'll have to do this in Sundown," Hawk explained to Strider, the horse breathing loudly through thick lips. "She's going to lose most of her protection there. There's no chance here. We must ride ahead and be ready for when she's finished her trip."

They were the same drunks that had passed Hawk earlier, and they were too busy shoving each other to notice the smeared paint across his face. They looked at each other, screwing their faces up, as Hawk rode away.

"Was he talking to that horse?"

"Yeah, something about a turnip."

CHAPTER

ELEVEN

"How did you fit all this in here?" Jacobi looked around the wagon's interior like a child staring at new toys.

Among the bed, wardrobe, desk, chests, and table with chairs, shelves were lined with old tomes that appeared forgotten. But it didn't smell like musty old books inside the caravan. Instead, the aroma was like being back at the ancient trees of Hawk's camp. Exotic trinkets that conjured images of strange and unknown things were strewn about, oddities against the flickering light of burning candles. There were a few instances of the same symbol appearing on books and ornaments as the one that hung about Jacobi's neck.

"That's only in your mind's eye," the magician smiled, twirling his moustache. He waved toward the table. "M'Laddo, would you care for a delicious cup of tea?"

Before Jacobi could answer, the cat returned with Rusty following through the small lower door within the larger door.

"Have you finished playing harrier with our guest?" Lafayette asked the animal.

The black cat raised its sleek head, eyes bright yellow with delight, slinking around Jacobi's leaning crutch before padding under the table.

"This elegant rascal is known as *Memphis*," Lafayette informed. "That feline would have one believe that he is some class of bounty hunter with the way he pursues that dog. One would not be incorrect to say that he has used more than nine of his precious lives during his mischievous proclivities."

"Pleased to meet you, *Memphis*," Jacobi nodded, reaching for the elusive cat. "How old is he, have you had him long?"

"Longer than you could well imagine, M'Laddo."

Rusty stayed near the door, panting slightly from the good time had, with his tongue hanging out as though he were smiling.

This dog really could smile.

Jacobi was sure of it.

When Memphis then sprang onto the bench, Jacobi realised that he hadn't noticed the chinaware teapot there earlier. A contrasting object in this peculiar tome and trinket-filled cabin on wheels, the pot a pure white with blue murals of dragons. Such an odd thing to have missed with its steam rising from a graceful spout.

The stranger thing was that there was no apparatus inside to have heated the water and there had been no campfire going outside.

Lafayette went to the teapot almost as soon as Jacobi had laid eyes upon it. "Most lovely, is it not? A beautiful design from our friends of the East."

"Back East, like Boston-way," Jacobi asked, "like where I am from?"

"Not at all, M'Laddo. East of our world, the *Orient*, as some may say."

That was farther than Jacobi really knew of. So much farther.

"Do you take sugar in your tea?"

"Actually," Jacobi answered, "I drink coffee, if you have it. Hawk made me some coffee that..." He didn't know how to finish describing that glorious brew.

"Was like no other," the magician politely completed the description.

Lafayette brought the teapot to the table with two matching patterned chinaware teacups. "Jacobi Nicholson. M'Laddo. We are not common reprobates, and we will not be consuming that putrid broth. As we will be discussing matters of Fate, we may as well begin with your *Boston Tea Party*. That event transpired over a century ago and the subsequent revolution was well and truly won. Years of transpiring Fate, you see, M'Laddo, have branded you with your Bostonian patriotism against tea. It is long overdue for retirement."

"I, uh...have no particular thing...against tea...I just like coffee."

"We will drink tea as civilised gentlemen in this otherwise uncivilised land. *Thus is Fate.*"

The magician studied the familiar charm around Jacobi's neck. "A passing glance with regard to your dishevelled state would lead the casual observer to think that Fate has been most unkind to you, Jacobi Nicholson. But a more trained study would see that it appears not to be the case, for Fate has indeed been kind to you. While you are not the first distressed soul that Hawk, Alfred Miller or Royce Falco have been charitable towards, you are the first to be delivered directly to me in this manner."

"What...*manner* is that?"

"You have been delivered wearing the pendant of Hawk's brother." Lafayette poured the tea and handed Jacobi a cup. "Why is that? That of itself begs curiosity."

Jacobi sipped the black tea, surprised by how much he enjoyed the sweetened flavour despite there being no sugar cubes in sight.

He began the tale of travelling from Boston into the West with Francis Geddes for a big adventure—he even included years of backstory, from his parents' death, to being taken in by the Geddes, to being betrothed to Gertrude, to being unable to have breathing space away from Francis.

The magician's intense blue gaze focused upon Jacobi, much as it had on the luxurious paddle steamer.

Then, after swallowing too much tea, Jacobi told of those he had heard and then saw in the sky on the night he fought with his friend. Of when he fell overboard from the paddle steamer into the maw of the Trikuhl and the Terrorgators and was saved by those spirits on horses and a thundering bird with barbarian archer at their lead. Then, upon waking in a world that felt far more real, the same man from the fever dream among the riders had handed him the necklace with the charm of intricate weaved lines. Not only that, but he had told Jacobi his sacred name that was known only to a special few.

"You see, M'Laddo, that talisman you wear around your neck, what do you know of it?"

Jacobi scratched his head while sipping more tea. "Hawk said it was a symbol for *Fate*. That I'd come to understand it."

"Allow me." Charles Lafayette refilled Jacobi's cup. "Understand that this knowledge isn't just bandied around like some common folklore. It is real. Most folk know that there must be something beyond their mortal selves, but life in general can't allow them to accept such a fancied destiny or magical thinking—

that we could all be bound toward some unified destination just sounds absurd to them. The symbol represents the Web of Fate. Those inter-weaving lines are a visual representation of something far grander than you and I alone. They represent *Mysterium*."

Charles Lafayette was raising his hands as though they were doing the explaining for him. Jacobi repeated the new word under his breath as the white gloves moved and weaved with practiced precision.

"*Mysterium* is...*Time*...*Space*...*Thought*...the web is it represented as a construct, but it is a natural construct, just as a tree growing and sprouting branches. All Fate is created by those that weave it. Every decision you make, every act you take, sets in motion a series of events in the strands of *Fate*—these are the *Scions of Fate*. Everything we do, all of us together, as one, is a consequence of our own devising coming together as one *Grand Unity*. We are the builders of our own Destiny. Masters of Fate."

"It sounds like magic..."

"Ah, M'Laddo, but of course. Remove the illusions and distractions. Is this all not what one would consider magic? Are we not the scions of since-passed sorcerers? You were involved or would be involved in every decision, whether of your will or against it or unknowing of it, that led to your falling into the Rubicon River."

"You were there, so that means you were involved!"

"Indeed. More than you would know." Lafayette sipped his own tea, wiping a little from his moustache, his eyes so alive with his performance. "There are many paths already taken, currently taking, and yet to take. Time, M'Laddo, is not always as it seems. What we have done, or choose to do, can even affect Fate going backward through time. Rewriting what you thought you knew."

"Rewriting time?"

"Yes indeed. It is rare to find a soul that can comprehend such an enigma." Lafayette appeared pleased that Jacobi was able to grasp the concept. "This may not be the first time you and I have actually sat here having this discussion. You see, M'Laddo, the creature that attempted to take you, some among their sinister kindred are able to unweave time, in essence, resulting in a re-weaving of time. They attempt to make reality bend to their will. Numerous times they have already done this. I can assure you that some modern conveniences should not be as readily available as they are. Cased ammunition and typewriters spring to mind immediately. Even something as simple as cola has emerged before its time."

"Geez," Jacobi could barely comprehend all of what he was being told. "What else?"

"I'll never be able to list them all, and some things are better left unknown, but, do you care for a Chunk?"

"Of what?"

"The chocolate bar," Lafayette smiled. "Do you care for a Chunk bar?"

"Love them!"

"There was a time when such a confection didn't exist, a time when you had never heard of such a treat."

"You sound so much like how some of my favourite stories read. The ones where someone travels to another time. Medieval knights, ancient Egypt, feudal Japan, pirates of the High Seas, or the American Revolution. I could go on."

"Ah, but our tales are not the sort of storybook you purchase for a dime at the general store for a cheap thrill. In our tale, you are bound to a great power that you have yet to understand. Those that can spin Wyrd, can see the threads of Fate weaving, and all those possibilities that could result through time. When you master this, you will be able to tempt Fate or flow with Fate as though it were water and bring about the destiny you wish to create. When the river of Mysterium flows not around you, but with you, you will be riding the Thunder Road."

"What does that mean for me?"

"Hawk sensed more in you than you know of yourself, and as Royce so claimed you have within yourself a budding talent to spin Wyrd. These new colleagues of yours are headed towards a convergence of Fate, whether it be for good or ill. Often is the case that they head towards ill upon the Thunder Road when they don't tread carefully. But trust me, M'Laddo. Because of this, I am humbled to offer my services to you for a future appointment, upon a single condition…"

Jacobi felt as though the room darkened, just as he thought it had on the *River Grace*.

"If ever you feel Fate converging, that you can sense that convergence to the point of *Doom*...then, you may call upon me."

Jacobi tried to follow just what that implied.

"Know that the Ghost Riders are tortured souls beyond redemption, cursed with forever pursuing an infernal herd across the eternal skies of Mysterium. The Thunder Road, for them, is cursed with no escape. Legend has it that the riders are a warning, that a time of reckoning is at hand, with failure resulting in riding the sky among their great hunt without end."

Lafayette's blue eyes pierced Jacobi's soul. "Oftentimes, a Ghost Rider is oblivious that their damnation while living led them to an eternal unlife. They did not heed the warnings that they had in life. Choices in Fate, you see. Why, I do wonder, did you see Hawk among them...and, before all else could possibly be answered, why did the Ghost Riders appear to you that fateful night?"

"I don't know..."

"*Thus is Fate...*" The magician produced a deck of cards, the top card's back bearing an image of three ravens. "We're going to discover just how well you can spin Wyrd."

CHAPTER

TWELVE

The wagon rolled in, passing the first sign that had been erected before this town was founded as Mudflats. It read:

THE PROMISED LAND

Miller breathed happiness at the sign. "Now we're talking, Royce. Mudflats. What a town!"

There was always a real sense of community in Mudflats. Sure, it was often wet—hence the name and the surrounding swampland—but the people were bound together with a township pride.

THUNDER ROAD

It was the sort of town that Alfred Miller could call *home* one day when his tired bones couldn't live with the constant riding on the fringes of civilisation any longer.

Royce had already cantered in on Firefly, being sure to tip his hat toward any clusters of women.

Some recognised him.

And Royce liked it that way.

As Rusty ran off to a group of small children, Miller was about to explain to Jacobi that Mudflats was founded by a wagon-train of freed slaves that made a harrowing journey from the north of Texas in 1865 to the south of Takoda Territory. Then he remembered that the young man wasn't sitting next to him—he'd been left in the care of Charles Lafayette.

There were many fires burning around the wet town. Near the middle, in front of the chapel, burned a large bonfire with a gathering of townsfolk, including dancers, singers, and musicians. The sound of the joyful song relaxed his heart.

This was a place where Miller learned to cope with the guilt of being a part of the Civil War. He had been conscripted into the South because that's where he lived. He didn't like it, but that's the way it was—but it still left him with an awful feeling that he knew would probably be with him until the day he died.

"Mister Miller!" called a voice that was happy to see the veteran. "And Mister Falco, too!"

"Bayard Clifton," Miller waved."

Royce tipped his hat to their old friend, a gesture that was instantly returned.

Bayard exemplified the people of Mudflats. Straw hat. Wheat hanging loosely from his mouth. A dedicated smile no matter how hard the work was. He was one of the free people that had made the journey from Texas.

This new life was picturesque and unmolested—the modern civilisation of Back East hadn't caught up to change their way of life. Yet. There was a sense that Mudflats was on borrowed time, but for now they lived with complete freedom.

Bayard came to the side of Miller's wagon, reaching up to shake his hand. "I hope you'll see me first, Mister Miller, if you're selling goods. I had some good runs on my stage business, and I'd be willing to share."

THUNDER ROAD

Miller pulled in beside a market stall that acted as the cheap façade of Bayard Clifton's stagecoach business.

CLIFTON EXPRESS

The sign may have only been a painted bedsheet stretched tight between two poles in the ground, but it caught the mild breeze with the same gentle pride that its owner displayed.

Miller parked the wagon parallel to a resplendent stage coach, also signed with the *Clifton Express* motif, that was in no way as cheap as the stall.

Bayard looked over what wasn't covered, giving a satisfied whistle. "Looks like Mister Hawk has been busy crafting again."

"He sure has," answered Miller. "We're pressed for time as we think Hawk is about to do himself a mischief that we'd rather be there to help prevent. We've got a young man with us, well, he's actually with Chuck Lafayette outside of town, but we need to pick him up."

"Mister Lafayette," Bayard was surprised, "outside Mudflats. Well, I'll be. He never gave us a visit or even let us know he was nearby."

Miller shook his head with practiced anguish. "Who actually knows with Chuck. He does what he does for reasons unknown to the rest of us."

"Well, Mister Miller, Sir—"

"I've told you, don't be calling me, *Sir*."

"Mister Miller—"

"And for the last time, drop the *Mister*."

"All right," Bayard yielded. "Here's what I can do. I'll buy as much as I can and help you sell the rest around town. Mudflats makes good coin selling African and Indian trinkets to the white folks passing through. Could take a day, though."

"We don't have a day." Miller thought a moment. "Royce, get over here and water the horses."

Royce had been talking with three young women in the shade of a rooftop, spinning a revolver on his finger at various angles to show off and impress. "Oh, that's Cranky Pants, I gotta go." He tapped the brim of his hat to part ways towards Miller, the women giggling together behind him.

Royce unburdened Sarge and Maple Stirrup, gathering them with Firefly to a horse trough and fetched some fresh water.

Water wasn't difficult to find around Mudflats.

Miller hatched a plan. "Are you free tonight, to run express from Mudflats to Sundown?"

"I can be. I'd just have to organise the wife and children."

"Royce," Miller beckoned. "I've been thinking..."

"Geez," Royce laughed to Bayard as he approached, "don't hurt yourself."

Miller almost ignored him, "Diggedd," then explained, "Bayard can take you and Jack, once Chuck is finished gawd-knows-what mystical malarkey with him, to Sundown. Tonight. Through the night. Try and beat Hawk to his own game. I'll stay overnight and sell the rest of Hawk's goods over the next day, hopefully find something else to buy here and then sell it in Sundown and meet you there as soon as I can."

"I can help with both of those things." Bayard was pleased. "You can stay in my barn, Mister Miller, it'll be empty while I have the Express out. You'll just need to muck out the stalls."

As Royce made a face of silent laughter at Miller—more for him having to do the job of cleaning up after horses rather than continually being called *Mister*—Bayard added, "And old Freeman just finished a batch of moonshine. He'd be eager to sell."

"Mudflats 'shine. Fantastic. Love this place," Miller said. "Let's all get started right now."

CHAPTER

THIRTEEN

As the stage coach rolled ever on, Jacobi took in the sights of all that...nothing. But that nothing was certainly something. Untouched virgin wilderness. Out here in this part of the West, proper civilisation was a long way from catching up. It was trying to, but it hadn't yet.

Royce and Jacobi had parted ways with Miller, boarding a stage coach headed express to Sundown. The plan was for Miller to stay in Mudflats and sell all the goods while the other two tried to reach Hawk in Sundown, and if their Native friend wasn't there they would perhaps try and meet him closer to Rosewood. And that was whether Hawk wanted them to or not. Then Miller would meet up with them in the wagon, hopefully full of something else to sell for a profit in Sundown.

This was the way Jacobi understood the plan.

Miller had handed Jacobi some coins and paper money for his assistance in the wagon delivery. "People are mostly scared of the Indians, but those Back East will pay big for their trinkets. Here's your cut. Hawk would want you to have it. It's only *proper*." The veteran had smiled at Royce with the last word.

The driver, Bayard Clifton, was the sole owner, operator and protector of the Clifton Express stagecoach service. It was a one-man stage business that he operated out of Mudflats. Opportunities were slim for the people of Mudflats, most of them adjusting to life as free people since the War ended. So, most made their own work. Like Bayard.

The savvy business owner had found an old stage bogged in the mud—a treasure of the swamp—and brought it back to life. Through good decisions and chance, he acquired four horses and was ready to cut across the

American West. And so, for a reasonable fee, Bayard will get you where you need to go.

Royce and Jacobi were the only two passengers, which Royce especially enjoyed. He spent most of the daylight hours snoozing on the plush red seat with his bowler hat over his face. That wild mane of platinum hair pillowed his head.

Fugg me, Jacobi thought, the man's hair is white no matter how much Miller denies it.

Royce had only asked a few questions about Lafayette. One was, "Are you questioning everything you thought you knew about the world?"

To which Jacobi answered, "Yes, indeed. It's a whole new world."

And the other was, "Did he tell you that you've got Wyrd?"

"Sort of, but not like that," Jacobi replied. "You seem to know a lot of how it went already."

"Because, long ago, he said the same sort of things to me."

"I thought I saw you spin...Wyrd."

"You saw me spin Wyrd?"

"Yeah," Jacobi nodded. "You made a Two of Clubs turn into an Ace of Skulls at Lafayette's wagon."

"You noticed that?"

"Yep."

"You noticed the Skull suit?"

"Yep"

"No wonder Hawk saw something in you."

Before Jacobi could ask about that, Royce gave him a deck of cards and had said, "Well, now that you're a regular Wyrdo, you can have this. But don't practice anything until we're in Sundown. Or better yet…maybe wait until we're out of Sundown. And whatever you do, Greenhorn, don't *tempt* Fate.""

"Will do."

"I'll tell you one thing that we're definitely doing when we reach Sundown."

"What's that?"

"Getting you some proper threads so you don't have to wear those shredded rags."

Jacobi smiled. "But I've almost gotten used to these."

"Nah, no more bloodied torn fancy Boston shid. We'll get you looking ace-high."

With that, Royce had slid the hat over his face and trusted in the protection of their driver.

It was a relatively uneventful trip.

Until the night fell, that is.

The horses were travelling erratically and there were howls in the distance that woke Jacobi. Royce had stayed awake. Bayard called that there was nothing to worry about, "Just a pack of wolves running alongside."

Jacobi had heard a wolf howl a few times while travelling West. He said to Royce, "That doesn't sound like any ordinary wolf..."

"You'd be right, Greenhorn."

It was a guttural howl that bellowed into the night.

They could both see out the window under the faint moonlight that there were the forms of hairy creatures running alongside the stage in the trees. They were just farther enough from the vehicle's lamplight to shroud them in darkness, but close enough to see that the wolves were the size of people that ran on all fours with a strange powerful gait.

Royce pulled another deck of cards from his pocket, slipping five cards into his left hand and drawing his revolver with the other.

As he leaned out the window of the stage, the cards lit up in his hand, the glow of fire radiant against his face and white hair and the steel of his revolver.

"You lot out there don't want to trouble yourselves with this stagecoach. In this hand, I'm holding a highly modified Holt Mustang '58 revolving pistol with 5 silver rounds chambered. And in this hand, I'm holding a winning poker hand hotter than the best bordello on nickel night. These ten things all have your names on them. I don't much want to waste any silver bullets or such a winning hand, and I don't care much for the smell of burnt fur, but needs must when the devil drives and all that hooey."

Bayard kept pushing the horses on.

It only took a few seconds for the running shadows to peel away and become lost within the night, their howls fading.

"Good job, Mister Falco, Sir," Bayard called. "Not a bullet wasted."

"It's Royce, remember. Mister Falco is my father."

"*Yessir*, Royce, Sir."

"I give up." Royce leaned back inside. "That reminds me, Greenhorn..."

"Of what?" Jacobi was still half terrified by the things that had been running alongside their stage. If he didn't know any better, he'd have sworn they were werewolves right out of the pages of his dime novels.

"We also gotta get you a shooting iron. I can't keep lending you my spare when it's time to save Miller's life."

"With silver bullets?"

"Was my bluff that good? My poker face?"

"What...? I couldn't see your face—it was out the window."

"Oh. Well. Right. Anyways. I don't actually have any silver bullets..."

PART IV

EDGE OF VENGEANCE

CHAPTER

FOURTEEN

Jacobi enjoyed the frontier cattle town of Sundown. It was busy. But not the same sort of busy that he disliked Back East.

Boston was rigid.
Sundown was loose.
Boston was tall, blocked the light, cold.
Sundown was low, let in light, warm.

There was no clip-clop of horseshoes on hard surfaces. That metallic clang against cobblestone didn't happen here. The graceful animals stepped quietly on a street of well-trodden dirt. This town was bustling with horse traffic, pulled wagons, their owners and working dogs. It was a sanctuary for cowboys and cattle drivers alike.

Jacobi had himself some hot coffee in a pale stone goblet that the bartender had explained was, "alabaster." As he ate his meal of meat and potatoes, he plucked another metal pellet from his teeth and placed it aside with the other two. The food in Sundown was served with a little less class than the manicured cuisine of Boston, but it was hearty and also fed the soul and that made all the difference.

He found himself wishing that he had some more of Lafayette's tea—or better yet, some of Hawk's coffee. Jacobi swore that between the magician's brew and the Indian's medicine that he'd recovered from his terrible wounds faster than expected.

Although Royce had said they'd find him some new clothes and a shooting iron, he had instead sent Jacobi into the saloon alone. "Don't pick a fight in there," Royce had said. "Don't let anyone pick a fight with you. And don't draw the spare iron I lent you. And don't try your cards yet. Just act casual until I get back. And Greenhorn...don't act like a greenhorn."

"Casual? Don't? What? What about getting me fixed with clothing and my own gun?"

"Later..."
"Well, where are you going?"
"I'm off to Miss Kitty's!"
"Who's that?"
"She's a pro...proprietress."
"A what?"
"She, uh, runs the *Scratching Post*."
"What's that?"

Jacobi didn't get another answer as Royce had sprinted down the street like a man on a mission.

Jacobi was tired and famished from the long coach journey. It hadn't been uneventful, that was for sure, and sleep had been difficult after what could only be described after the matter as western werewolves.

His entire going West had been eventful.

One big event after another.

But, after his meal, it would be time to ditch the torn Boston clothes and find those new frontier threads for living in the West. With or without Royce's help.

"But none of that Boston shid," Jacobi remembered Royce saying.

For living in the West.

Living...?

Or surviving?

For *surviving* in the West.
This Wild West.
This Wyrd West.
To survive this Wyrd Wild West.

Maybe he'd have some luck trying to locate Hawk when he got the chance to wander around Sundown. He wanted to thank the man for saving his life and find out on Miller's behalf if he was about to do something he'd regret.

They were good people he'd met. First the enigmatic Hawk, then the no-nonsense Alfred Miller and the impulsive Royce Falco. And finally, the mysterious Charles Lafayette. Jacobi had found himself their welcome stranger in their unwelcoming strange land.

He was here. One of Royce's favourite places in the world. He hadn't seen the world, but he knew this would be one of his favourite places no matter what. It was far enough from the eyes of the main street of activity and the church, but not far enough that getting here wasn't worth it. It was close enough for a quick skip to, but not as far as the stink of the pig pens.

The sign filled him with delight every time he saw it. Scarlet letters on black, a horseshoe at both ends upturned to catch luck.

SCRATCHING POST

Felines of all varieties caressed the tall red house. Their claw marks were evident on the boards of the bordello, this only partly responsible for the namesake of the place. They had every kind of house cat here. All that was missing was some sort of great big wild cat.

"Royce Falco," breathed a sultry voice. "Do my eyes deceive me?"

"Miss Kitty," Royce responded to the brunette woman leaning out of the third-floor window, her bodice barely containing her endowment. "Who else could it be?"

"Oh, you know, some other red-haired rascal. You cowpokes are all so hard to tell apart."

"That stings me, Miss Kitty. Surely, I stand out from the crowd..."

Her answer was a knowing smile.

THUNDER ROAD

Royce entered the building, coming into the vestibule. Cats preened themselves and rubbed along his legs as he saw a large poster of Rosette Kimble, the famed singer, adorning one of the walls. The poster was from her 1869 tour when it stopped for two weeks in La Grande. The woman on the poster had it all, the face and voice to enthral the theatres—Royce knew that she even had the chest and legs to get by in a place like this if she ever changed profession. Royce took the bowler from his head and placed it on a hat rack beside some other hats of those already partaking of the Scratching Post's offerings.

When he entered the establishment's foyer proper, he was greeted by name from many familiar welcoming faces.

Inside the rustic Sundowner Saloon—called *The Sundowner* by locals—Jacobi had himself a fantastic view. He was seated at a table close to the piano being played, accompanied by another on banjo, while being able to look out the window across the paddocks, corrals, and pens of Sundown. He dined alone, trying not to draw any attention to his battered and bruised self, as the warming midday sun passed over the livestock town.

For the first time since going West, Jacobi felt that perhaps he could start to feel relaxed. There were no ghostly voices here, no half-man half-spider all-nightmare monsters, no werewolves, and there didn't appear to be any misguided militia about.

Sundown was a busy sort of peaceful.

But it didn't last long.

Just as he noticed three ravens in a row, each perched upon its own telegraph pole, a familiar red and white dog rushed across some paddocks toward the saloon. The red husky was sniffing a trail, most likely Royce's and his own. Had Rusty followed the coach through night and day? Through that howling territory? The dog rushed under the swinging saloon doors, bending towards Jacobi. Rusty barked in time with a haunting chant that had become suddenly apparent, a rising ghostly chorus he'd heard before he fell from the *River Grace...*

CHAPTER

FIFTEEN

"I will wear my hair long." Hawk had walked with deliberate pace from the brush surrounding Sundown, leaving his faithful horse, Strider, behind to graze on some lush green grass.

Passing some homesteads unnoticed, avoiding line of sight with anyone, he had made his way toward the rear of Sundowner Saloon. He knew this town. It was very familiar. "I am known by the name of my people. Behold! The *Horse Nation*. Dancing! Proudly they come. I am Red Hawk of the Takoda."

Hawk's long feather-bound black hair flowed behind him. His face was still streaked with red and black paint. Bare shoulders revealed smudged white dots upon his tan skin. The painted red bird mural had been touched up across his chest. He was barefoot, the only clothing worn were buckskin pants.

Some townsfolk finally noticed him. They scattered upon seeing a savage entering Sundown! It was a rare sight since most of the wild Takoda Indians had been forcibly removed from the surrounding areas. If the sight of a warpainted savage didn't strike fear into the populace of Sundown, then the tomahawk in his hand sure did. The Indian walked with indomitable steps, ignoring the fleeing civilians, and entered one of the rear doors of Sundowner Saloon.

"Hey," a cowboy gasped, "you don't belong in here!"

"This Fate is not for you." Hawk raised the tomahawk, brushing the man aside. "Do not choose to make it so."

The cowboy didn't even put a hand to his holstered revolver. Instead, he dropped his drinking glass and ran for the door. "Get the Law. There's an Indian in here!"

Hawk made his way up the stairs, passing fleeing patrons as he read the brass plate on each door that he passed. He stopped at the one room he sought above any other.

Hawk had successfully stalked the Gold Baroness of the West undetected for years. The opportunity to enact vengeance upon her for her crimes against the land and its people would be easily calculated. When the day came, he knew Fate would show him just where and at what moment to strike. With the arrival of the Boston boy, Fate had shown clearly that Twyla Matthias' day had drawn near.

Her guards had headed toward the train station, and all signs of opportunity told that the saloon was the place and that the time had arrived.

One of Twyla Matthias' many habits were flaunting her gold and renting rooms, whether saloon or bordello. Loose lips of townsfolk around Sundown—that weren't aware of an Indian in their midst—had gossiped of "Room 9."

When he reached the room, Hawk smashed the door open, wood splintering around the handle. A man and two women—in various stages of undress—were with Twyla Matthias.

He pointed the tomahawk with menace at his target to remain but spoke to her guests. "Cover your shame and go with peace," the Indian commanded. They scrambled for as much of their clothing as the most direct route to the door would allow.

Twyla Matthias had already been redressing, adjusting her brunette hair about her bare shoulders. Her usually porcelain face appeared as though she had been in a state of hurried bother before Hawk had arrived. "What is the meaning of this?" she demanded.

Hawk sensed the same flittering shadow about her as he did in Rosewood. But it did not matter, whatever that was would suffer the same consequence as her—Trikuhl or not.

"I *was* Thunder Hawk of the Takoda." The Indian stomped over to the woman as she reached under her carmine dress for a concealed weapon. "Your greed ends here." He knocked the knife that she had produced from a garter across the room. "For my people that you displaced and the spirits of those you murdered, for the entire Horse Nation. For the land that you rape of gold and aetron that you cannot eat." She reached for her military sabre that lay on a ruffled bed, but that was also knocked away before it could even be withdrawn from its scabbard.

"I-I remember you...from one of the groups that refused to move to the Reservation." Twyla raised her hands, attempting to pass the blame for the atrocities committed. "It was Captain Cordell that attacked the Takoda."

"Funded by your blood-stained gold and your need for more!" Hawk swung his axe with the head angled so the blunt flat bulk of it would be enough to drop the woman to the floor. She was good, she knew how to fight and defend herself, but Hawk had the element of surprise and years of honing his skills in the wild.

He grabbed a clump of tousled hair, dragging his prey from the room to an adjoining doorway that led to the balcony outside.

Most townsfolk near the back of The Sundowner had initially scattered, but some had returned and headed toward the front. Others also gathered in the street below the balcony, having heard the spreading word about the savage Indian across town. This included Jacobi, restraining Rusty.

Hawk stood behind Twyla Matthias, facing her to the townspeople, forcing her to her knees at the balcony railing. He then placed the sharp edge of the tomahawk across the top of Twyla's forehead, pressing, drawing blood, ready to scalp the woman that had been a stain upon the land.

He drew his victim's head back enough to gaze into her eyes, to watch the evil slip away when the time came—but Twyla offered no resistance as the sharp edge dug a little farther into her scalp.

"What...what are they?" she cried. "Who are they?"

Something was vastly different in her eyes, as though she was seeing a terrifying world beyond. The woman's gaze darted around, not at the townsfolk below, but at many things in the air that were not there. "I'm sorry, forgive me..." She didn't possess the terror of waiting inevitably to die; she wasn't even offering any resistance for her life.

And the flittering shadow, that dark haze about her, was gone.

Twyla peered with horror all about herself, surrounded by a swarm of terrible things greater than the threat of death.

"Please," she begged, but not to the Indian, "forgive me for what I have done."

Jacobi had heard them approaching, just as Twyla had before Hawk burst into her room. Ghost riders, formless spirits of ghastly men and horses, circled about Sundowner Saloon. They fired guns of smoke and hollered unholy things. Hawk's face had become like a skull, his hair aflame. Burning wings appeared to sprout from the Indian's back as a great storming bird arrived to perch behind him. Jacobi realised that only he and Hawk's victim were witnessing the spectral occurrence. The townsfolk only saw a savage threatening a well-known damsel.

And there it was...

Behind a helpless Twyla.

Behind the emblazoned Hawk.

A semi-formed black spider-thing.

Hawk continued to hold Twyla Matthias as something unknown other than he and the tomahawk continued the torment. As her head came farther back he saw the monster in the reflection of her eyes.

He felt it.

She could only watch as her personal angel of death, the demonic visage of the

THUNDER ROAD

Indian, swung the tomahawk away from her scalp and into the black many-red-orbed inky form in one motion.

There was a visceral squelch as an emerald liquid spat from the wispy form. The monster emitted a high pitched shriek and reacted by swinging a couple of its black skeletal limbs at Twyla and Hawk, smashing them across the balcony.

The townspeople were confused.

They were confused and afraid.

All they appeared to see was the savage Indian withdraw his axe for a better swing, but he'd dropped it, and it flung with momentum over the crowd watching below as Twyla was released. Some wondered if it was possible that she'd bested the savage?

Jacobi witnessed the ethereal hoard disappear with the weapon and the Trikuhl scramble away up a wall and over the Sundowner's rooftop. It really didn't like being wounded or under the sun.

Not that it would have mattered amongst the folk of Sundown that the Indian hadn't continued his assault, but it came all too late as a revolver shot from a lawman running in the street found the Indian's chest.

Deputies spilled out onto the balcony, overpowering and beating the painted savage as Twyla Matthias continued to cower in terror.

They kicked the Indian back into the saloon and down the stairs. The Law continued the assault as they came out into the street and towards the Sheriff's Office. The people of Sundown threw vegetables at the savage Indian from the displays of market stalls, cussing at him, as he was dragged brutally on.

Jacobi had held Rusty through the ordeal. He dropped his crutch and, with a limp, retrieved the tomahawk with the green goo on its blade before anyone began to care enough about it. He continued to hold the barking husky's fur outside the crowd, trying to calm him and keep him from going after Hawk— he'd heard how bad it could be to end up on the dog's bad side.

"Go and find Royce." Jacobi held Rusty's fur to face him directly, looking intently into the dog's different coloured eyes. "Do that thing you do. Then bring him back here. Do you understand? Find Royce! Lead Royce here!"

THUNDER ROAD

Jacobi looked up at Twyla Matthias cowering from the unseen terrors, nobody able to get close enough to the flailing woman to help her. Twyla shouted to be left alone, going inside and pulling the door to her room shut.

As Rusty bolted away, Jacobi waded through the crowd trying to reach Hawk. He shoved manic onlookers away. "You can't do this!" he shouted, tomahawk hidden, his voice drowned by the mob.

In time, Jacobi could only stand there upon his crutch, helpless, as Hawk was dragged violently into the Sheriff's Office. The door shut behind, muffling the screams of unnecessary brutality.

"Go, dog, go." Jacobi breathed, hoping Rusty would find Royce fast. "And where are you, Miller. We need you..."

Rusty's bark changed. He'd found a hatless Royce, the man's white hair ruffled, at the other end of the street. He was pulling his pants higher as he tried to fasten his belt, having mostly dressed himself at a hurried pace towards the commotion in town. He'd caught a glimpse of Hawk being beaten into the Sherrif's office and had drawn his revolver from his loose gunbelt.

Jacobi shook his head for Royce to not act—to not do anything foolish, to act causal—hoping Royce could keep his impulses in check.

Royce checked the ammunition in the cylinder of his weapon, looking like he wasn't going to take the advice. Jacobi held the tomahawk high quickly, hoping the weapon could somehow draw his attention to a calmer state. Upon seeing the Indian's axe, Royce placed his weapon back in its holster and walked toward Jacobi through the townsfolk.

The young man sighed with relief. There were just too many lawmen to cause any further trouble. Well, Jacobi wasn't good at causing trouble, but he knew Royce could if given even half of half-a-chance.

At Jacobi's end of the street, he spotted an unhitched horse with a golden-tan coat and black-striped legs. It was Strider. The horse that had brought Hawk here, and that had pulled Jacobi by travois into the West.

The horse had seen the entire ordeal.

CHAPTER

SIXTEEN

In Sundowner Saloon, Room 3, Jacobi had furtively cleaned and hid Hawk's unique weapon in the bottom drawer of the bedside dresser. That strange emerald liquid slid off the axe blade easily, leaving him to wonder if it was some sort of blood from the Trikuhl— and if the monster was still around. The tomahawk was strange to him, hollow through the handle to a small bowl-like opening at the poll opposite the blade.

As he closed the drawer, thinking about how Royce had needed to return to the Scratching Post to collect his hat that he'd left behind, there was a knock at the door.

"Who is it?" Jacobi asked, not expecting Royce back so soon.

"My name is...well, you know me," the voice was familiar, pausing before revealing, "...I'm Twyla Matthias..."

"Uh," Jacobi's skin turned an impossible shade of white, "I'm not expecting anyone by that name."

"I know it's you from the boat, young man—and I'm actually glad that you're okay." Her mannerisms were certainly different. Vastly different. "I saw you pick up the Indian's weapon outside."

After the incident with Hawk, he wasn't ready to deal with anything like that just yet. Despite all the madness of almost being scalped and surely witnessing an appearance by ghost riders, Twyla Matthias had seen him retrieve the tomahawk and had recognised him. She'd surely used her resources and cunning to find him—his name was signed into Sundowner Saloon's guest registry—and was undoubtedly coming to collect the debt that the dullard Francis had caused.

That's twice now his name was easily found. Jacobi realised he really needed to start using an alias in the West—perhaps *Jack* was becoming a good idea.

Jacobi opened the door. Why did I open the door? He knew he'd probably regret the decision.

If not for her already-established reputation, everybody around The Sundowner at the time of the attempted murder by the savage Indian recognised Twyla Matthias. Without a doubt, the woman who had almost been scalped upstairs outside Room 9 stood at his doorway.

Lavish red dress. Gold-plated revolver holstered with army sabre hanging from the same belt. Matching red bonnet held in manicured fingers that quivered. "I'm sorry to intrude. May I come in?"

This was not the Twyla Matthias that Jacobi and Francis had faced at the poker table on the *River Grace*.

Sure, her porcelain features had returned, and her dark hair was tied perfectly with a medical dressing in it, but it was the nervous hands that threw Jacobi's expectations off. Everything that he knew about the woman had come from Hawk, Miller, Royce, Lafayette and his own experience on the *River Grace*—

and not one piece of that information was pleasant.

"Please, do not fear," Twyla pleaded, "I am not here to collect on the debt. In fact, on my behalf, do consider the debt rescinded."

"Why would you do that?" Jacobi pointed to the professional wound-dressing adorning the area where a tomahawk had sliced into Twyla's hair and skin. "Did the axe cut too far into your head?"

Jacobi thought that remark may have been too far. While she was a dangerous person, she didn't seem dangerous now. Twyla was undeserving of sarcasm in the moment.

"If I may, I'd like to explain everything."

Jacobi looked throughout the hallway for any of her protective thugs. "Don't you keep guards anymore? Word is that you have thugs and soldiers in your employ."

Twyla explained. "I relieved them of their contract, stating that the Indian was clever enough to attack me when they were elsewhere in Sundown, so their services were useless to me. I sent them back to their commanding officer where they belong. It was an abuse of my standing to illegally engage the private services of U.S. Army soldiers from that rogue, Captain Cordell, for my own personal needs."

Jacobi had heard that name mentioned before by Miller, among many others. Twyla Matthias didn't appear to be the force of personality that he had first met, but perhaps this was for the better. She was letting go of things such as illegal mercenaries and expensive debts to stupid folk that were caught in a gambling trap—things that were unpleasant about herself.

Wanting to know Francis' consequences after the *River Grace* outweighed Jacobi's not wanting to know. Before he could ask about his absent travelling companion, Twyla explained, "I sent orders to Boom Town...to release your friend. Francis Geddes was to work off your shared debt to me in the mines there. He is free—you were presumed dead."

Jacobi said, "You've done a lot in a short time?"

"My heart has changed a lot in that short time," Twyla answered. "The Gold Baroness was just a front to survive in a man's world. A façade that took on a life of its own."

Jacobi breathed a sigh of relief, not just in part for himself, but at least knowing that

Francis could go. "I just hope that idiot can work out how to get Back East." Convinced of her, Jacobi motioned Twyla inside, closing the door behind.

"Listen to you, Boston Boy, acquiring the lingo."

Jacobi tried his first smile around Twyla. "Hot coffee?" He poured the beverage from a pot into the room's second alabaster goblet, handing it to Twyla, motioning for her to sit in a plain wooden chair.

"Thank you."

Jacobi sat on the end of the bed, sipping his own. "It's good and hot, but not as good as a coffee I tasted recently in the wild."

Twyla raised her goblet. "We're all discovering new things here." After tasting the beverage and releasing a smile of delight, Twyla began the story of why she had come to Jacobi.

"The Indian, this *Hawk*—or Red Hawk as he was known when he was rebelling against progress—may as well have stripped the scalp from my wicked head for what I have done in my time, especially to him and his people. He hesitated, and I know I risk all sincerity when I tell you this, I'm sure that he hesitated because he knew I was seeing something from Beyond."

Twyla Matthias met Jacobi's eyes, locking his gaze. "You see, Jacobi Nicholson, of Boston, Massachusetts, I could hear *them* approaching before Hawk arrived, before *they* arrived. As that axe you retrieved was brought to my skull, it was then that I saw the spirits of a thousand tortured riders flying from the sky, through my soul, their clarion call so deafening that I could no longer be as I once was. You see, as the Gold Baroness, I have witnessed the ghost riders many times before. Always haunting me to alter my ways. I even heard them on the *River Grace*. It wasn't until I was under the edge of that axe blade that I could take it no more. I know I must follow a better path...we," she motioned towards Jacobi and herself, "must free Hawk, if it's the least I can ever do for him."

"Lady." The door to the room swung completely open. Royce, finally returned, cocked the gun he pointed at Twyla Matthias' wounded head. "You're not even going to get the chance!"

CHAPTER

SEVENTEEN

A familiar bark made Jacobi sit more upright than he already was. Royce training his weapon's barrel at Twyla Matthias was already enough to keep him on the edge of his seat—well, edge of the bed where he sat.

Royce relaxed his aim a little, Rusty's bark almost like its own language.

Thoughts of Twyla's story of ghostly visitations that saved her life from Hawk's vengeful tomahawk faded from Jacobi's mind. As curious as those strange events certainly were, he was left wondering why he had witnessed—now for the second time—the ghost riders before they made an appearance to the terrified Twyla Matthias.

"You go, Greenhorn. Sounds like Miller might be in town." Royce uncocked the hammer of his revolver and holstered it. "Instead of a bullet, me and Matthias are gonna have ourselves a little chat."

Jacobi dashed outside to the balcony—the same balcony that was almost host to a scalping—leaning on the balustrade to see Rusty signalling toward him, as only a dog can.

On the worn road alongside the paddocks and pens came the grizzled Alfred Miller driving Maple Stirrup and Sarge from upon a wagon loaded with barrels.

Jacobi rushed—past his room where the scene still looked peaceful—down through the hotel as best his healing limp would allow with the crutch. Dodging a passing stagecoach, he reached Miller.

"Rusty found you!" He stroked the husky's face.

"He sure did, Jack," Miller answered. "Is there a reason why he's so antsy? Has Hawk actually gone and done what we think he was going to do?"

"Sort of." Jacobi bowed his head. "Almost."

"Fugg, I knew it," Miller sighed. "This good boy has a certain bark and dance of impatience when one of his friends is in trouble."

"Hawk stopped the scalping before the deputies had even got him."

"Why would he stop, when he finally had that fugging bidge's life in his hands?"

"The short version is that Twyla Matthias had a sudden moral epiphany about her life."

"Having an axe to your head'll do that!"

"It wasn't the axe." Jacobi was sincere. "She saw...*them*..."

"What...I don't believe it. Really?"

"It's true."

"You mean, she saw...*them*, as in...?"

Jacobi nodded, knowing Miller understood. "The ghost riders."

Miller shook his head with disbelief as he continued to remove the ropes from the barrels of moonshine.

"I saw them too," Jacobi added, "again."

Miller dropped the ropes with disbelief.

"I could hear them coming, like I did on the *River Grace*. They came for her at that moment before death, and Hawk seemed to understand something was going on with

Twyla and spared her. Since then, Twyla Matthias has changed. I haven't mentioned it yet, but I think there was also a Trikuhl..."

"Fugg me six ways to Sunday. I hear you, but why would you believe her; how do you know?"

"We met and she told me that she's turned over a new leaf."

"So where is she now?"

"Royce is upstairs. He was about to shoot her. But now she's his captive audience."

"So your new friend Twyla Matthias has seen ghost riders, and you can vouch that fact for her because you saw them as well? And now she's Royce's guest in the Sundowner? And there may be a Trikuhl about." Miller dusted his hat off after the revelation. "You seeing them too is about the only thing that would make me believe she's seen them and changed her ways."

Jacobi let the story sink in some more before adding, "Twyla wants to help us to try to get Hawk freed."

"I'll go to the Sherrif's office and see what I can do about having a go. Sometimes people have a soft spot for old veterans."

"But weren't you with the South?"

"Yeah, but I surrendered and swore allegiance to the Union Army and then fought on the Western Frontier, where I met Sarge here. I just don't usually tell anyone about the Southern part—not sure why I told you so early on." Miller grinned. "Problem is, if I can't do anything, we'll have to rely on Twyla Matthias' bribes and clout."

Miller put his hand on the delivery wagon. "Jack, while I'm gone, I need you to do your best to sell this 'shine to the saloon and get Stirrup and Sarge and the wagon stabled. This batch was meant to go to Rosewood, but it looks like it'll be staying in Sundown. I'll make sure that no Law comes this way while you make the sale. I can't promise I won't punch Twyla Matthias in the face if I see her, so that'll be one way I can keep the Law away from you."

"Won't somebody at Rosewood eventually want to know where their *'shine* is?"

"Always..." Miller began walking, answering back over his shoulder. "Consider it part of learning how life works here in the West."

PART V

SORCERER'S NIGHT

CHAPTER

EIGHTEEN

Jacobi Nicholson, Alfred Miller, Royce Falco and Twyla Matthias sat facing each other at a small round wooden table on the balcony of the saloon. One level off the ground, they were drinking the new moonshine from Mudflats that The Sundowner had recently acquired and had just began serving.

"What is on these?" Jacobi asked, holding a glazed peanut between his thumb and index finger. He felt like a new person. He had discarded his tattered old Boston tourist clothes for something that suited the cowboys of Sundown.

Under the coming twilight of the evening they politely declined the conversation of another saloon girl—much to Royce's chagrin as he explained to Jacobi that the nut was, "roasted in Canadian maple syrup."

Miller weighed their entire situation.

"You've certainly changed your tune, *Gold Baroness*. You went as far as trying to buy Hawk's life with gold. If not for your welcome interference, he would have probably already swung from the gallows for no other crime than being a fugging Indian. But now they're playing it all by the letter of the Law again. And you give us inside information. You seem different now. You know, before today, I could have happily put a couple of bullets in you."

Royce spoke over his glass, popping another peanut into his mouth. "I still could."

Twyla swallowed too much moonshine at the thought. "I am thankful nobody has." She turned to Miller. "But was hitting me across the face necessary?"

"You hit me first!" Miller responded, to which Twyla nodded an understanding.

Royce laughed.

"What's so funny," Twyla asked.

"You, Pretty." Royce answered. "That little spot of a bruise on your face will match the cut Hawk gave you up top. I'm sure you'll be able to accessorise it with the latest style from Paris."

"And you've had more than that coming your way for years," Miller answered, "and it was only to get the Sherriff and his boys' attention away from young Jack here."

"Ahem!" Royce's eyes widened at Miller.

"And Royce," Miller added reluctantly, "fancies himself an outlaw and keeps his company away from the Law where possible. But anyway, our bigger issue, we need to explain to Jack."

Jacobi listened attentively as Miller continued, despite the tasty nuts crunching in his mouth. "We have both run out of time and gained more time. Hawk may have avoided the noose by mob, but the time that has passed has allowed an old enemy of ours, Captain Cordell—"

"Fugghead," Royce slipped in a cuss.

"—to learn of Hawk's capture. The captain is already outside the limits of Sundown with more troops than we'd be able to count. Some of them were Twyla's. There's no way we can do any more for Hawk here. He will be escorted by the U.S. Army from Sundown to the Takoda Reservation up north.

But first, Cordell's going to detour east across the Rubicon River with Hawk to get even more troops from Fort Morgan before coming back over the river to then make their way north-west. Cordell has expressly stated that he wishes to escort the prisoner to the reservation with a show of military force as a message to the Indians there. Hawk is then to remain there for the rest of his natural life. Leaving will instantly put a bounty upon his head: dead or alive."

"I don't like it," Jacobi said. "I'm no soldier, but isn't that overly complicated?"

"I said the same, saying that Hawk could be accompanied by Sundown's Law instead straight to the reservation land. But this plan is going ahead." Miller wasn't happy. "This is personal for Captain Cordell. He wants to be recorded in history as responsible for conquering the rebellious Indians, the Horse Nation, from these lands."

Royce sat up. "Cordell's with Sicarius, and with that shadowy group there's always going to be more to it."

"What's that?" Jacobi asked, Twyla also interested.

"The Sicarius Assembly? A secret society pushing the darker agenda of *Manifest Destiny*. To drive the natives out, to settle the West—to *conquer* the West."

"Wouldn't surprise me if he was in some secret society. I know," Twyla revealed, but adjusted her statement with, "*I knew*, Captain Cordell well. But not well enough to know that. He was the sort of man that thought women had their place, and although I was well connected, I didn't have the right bits to be at his level."

Miller interrupted. "I served under the fugging bastard, for the Union."

Twyla absorbed that. "I doubt this elaborate plan is for Hawk's safety. In fact, I doubt Hawk will ever reach the Takoda Reservation. Cordell hates the Indians. He wants to see them crushed."

"Yep," Miller agreed, memories of his past surfacing, "he sure does."

Jacobi put his glass down. "These events, they're all tied together somehow in a way that's bigger than all of us. We need to do something...to save him."

"What, though?" Twyla was listening. "There's no way to spring him from that cell.

Money won't work and the army is near." She looked to Royce. "And one of your brothers is with them."

"Shid, no, which one. Not Kayne?"

"Victor."

"*Goggles*, eh? He could be a problem. We attack when Hawk's out of the cell, away from Sundown. Hopefully before most of the army meets the prisoner."

Miller had an idea. "They have to reach Fort Morgan. They'll need to use the bridge to cross the river. That's when they'll be vulnerable."

"But trapped on the bridge Hawk will probably be at his most vulnerable too." Jacobi suggested, "We need a trick—we need a distraction…"

"Oh no…" Miller sighed.

Royce grinned. "Oh yes…"

Jacobi was nodding, knowing Miller could sense where he was leading the conversation. "We get more weapons and ammo." The young man knocked his glass over like a chess piece with his revolver. "And, we get some help. Some real help."

"I'm in," Royce didn't need to hear any more, knocking his own glass over and placing his revolver on the table.

"Uh...who's help?" Miller sighed, knowing he shouldn't have asked.

"Lafayette." Jacobi placed his revolver on the table where his glass was. "He made me a deal."

Royce added, "And I know where he is."

"*Chuck the magician...?* That's your plan? And some more guns?" Miller was annoyed by the very existence of Lafayette, but he couldn't deny the man's strange abilities.

Twyla's curiosity piqued. "*Lafayette.* As in, *The* Charles Lafayette? The mysterious magician sitting at our poker table on the *River Grace*? The one that promised there'd be no magic with the deck?"

"Of course you've fugging met him too," Miller sighed, shaking his head.

Jacobi confirmed. "The very same."

"If Charles Lafayette is what we need," Twyla placed her gold-plated revolver on the table next to the others after knocking her own glass over, "then count me in."

"What?" Miller laughed. "There's no way you're coming."

"And why not?" Twyla demanded.

"Because you're a fugging woman!"

She scoffed, "What's that got to do with it?"

Jacobi raised a hand. "She's *someone* willing to help us free Hawk, and we could use all the help we can get."

Miller sank back in his chair, biting his tongue with thought for a moment. "Well, apparently, you've seen the ghost riders too. That's gotta count for something." He sculled his remaining moonshine. "You win, Jack. If anyone can pull the wool over the eyes of these soldiers *and* a Falco brother, it's Chuck *fugging* Lafayette."

He nodded at Twyla. "This kid is thinking like a real outlaw." Miller put his glass lip-down on the table and placed his revolver next to the other three. "Let's leave Sundown before any army arrives."

"So, we're doing this?" Jacobi smiled.

Miller put a firm hand on Jacobi's shoulder while they all retrieved their weapons, nodding. "Yes Jack, we're fugging doing this. But we better hurry: there's a storm coming."

No mistake about it. The approaching twilight was stained by the appearance of dark clouds.

Royce scraped the remaining maple glazed peanuts into a pants pocket, except one. That last one he flicked above his head into the air from his thumb, then caught it in his mouth on its way back down. He then stood, looking at the brewing clouds. "I've got a bad feeling about this..."

CHAPTER

NINETEEN

It had become dark quickly. Night had fallen, but the onset of twilight had come so fast. A coldness swept through Sundown and the stars were hidden. Livestock had been herded into corrals and barns, hay had been covered or moved, hatches had been battened, and the general populace of Sundown had scattered from the oncoming weather.

With an attempted murder by a savage and a coming storm, it had turned out to be one of the more interesting days in Sundown's recent history.

"Storm's coming on fast," Miller said as he loaded another box onto the back of the wagon while Rusty ran around pretending to be helpful.

Royce adjusted the brim of his hat. "I really don't like it. Something unnatural about the sky."

"Probably Lafayette's doing then, right?" Miller tapped the material of the wagon canopy. "Lucky that we put the cover up."

Royce chuckled. "Thought you didn't believe he could do that sort of thing?"

"Sometimes I want to believe, but it goes against my better judgement."

As Jacobi wrangled their horses, including Hawk's, Twyla heaved an old suitcase onto the wagon. "Looks like the last one."

"I told you, woman," Miller barked, "I'll load the wagon."

"You know, being a woman doesn't mean that I'm helpless."

"And just because I'm old doesn't mean I can't load my own wagon."

Royce stepped in. "Alright, alright. We're looking ready. Let the steam out of your engines, you two."

Twyla giggled which broke Miller's stoic veneer into a slight smile.

Miller took the reigns of the wagon while Jacobi rode shotgun, Twyla and Royce riding their horses while Hawk's was tethered to the back of the wagon.

They were being watched.
But they didn't know that.

As their little caravan pulled away from outside Sundowner Saloon, the watcher matched their pace on foot, having emerged from the shadows. The watcher would have the main road of Sundown all to themself, the townsfolk having fled for cover from the storm.

There wasn't an eye left to see it, but the watcher stood in the middle of the road at one end of town, arms raised to the sky. If there had been a witness left, they would have seen the black clad figure wearing a mask formed of feathers creating a cone, or more so, a beak. Twin ocular lenses covered the eyes under the hood of a cloak that was topped with a wide-brimmed hat, further hiding the watcher. In one hand was a black cane with a decorative grip. A dark cape billowed behind as the wind increased and the storm became stronger, appearing to be at the watcher's command.

With arms raised to the sky, the watcher welcomed the oncoming storm.

CHAPTER

⊕

TWENTY

"He's here." Royce was confident as the rain fell from the curled brim of his hat. "I *just* know it."

"He's toying with us, as usual," Miller grumbled. At a crossroads, two hours ride south of Sundown, a few dozen yards north of the ruined town of Haven, the veteran shook his head with frustration. "How do you even know he's here?"

Royce smiled—the smile of a man that thought he had the answers to all of life's questions. "You see, dear Miller, our mutual magician friend said to me before we left Mudflats to—Royce put on his best Lafayette impression—*find me south of Sundown where no one dare look* and I'm pretty sure that's here."

Miller didn't answer. "Jack, get me the shovel..."

By the light of the rain-spitting lantern hanging on the horse-drawn wagon that had been driven from Sundown, Jacobi rummaged for a shovel. "This place is giving me the creeps..." The rain clouds covering most of the night stars didn't help his feeling of anxious dread.

Miller smiled. "You don't know the half of it. Haven isn't called a *ghost town* just because it's empty and falling apart...it's *said* to be haunted..."

Jacobi could see the slight silhouettes of dilapidated buildings under the limited starlight—they were too close for comfort.

Twyla Matthias put down some wet hay and water from the wagon for their five horses, apologising to them. At least the tub for the water could refill itself from the weather while they were here. Maple Stirrup and Sarge had pulled the wagon while Hawk's horse, Strider, which Jacobi had stabled after seeing it in Sundown, was tethered to the back. Firefly was off doing his own thing, inspecting a tuft of green grass. "There you go, Dasher," Twyla stroked her brown and white horse.

Rusty shook vigorously, spraying rainwater in all directions from his fur, some of his human companions shielding their faces from the wet explosion.

The dog sniffed around to assist Jacobi with finding the shovel as the young man wondered, "Shouldn't there be that weird caravan-wagon thing of his nearby?"

"You'd be forgiven for thinking so, but this is fugging Chuck Lafayette we're talking about." Miller looked around, not expecting anyone to be passing by as the hour was approaching midnight, but explained what could happen. "Parts of the Frontier, like Haven, are more dangerous than others, especially at night. Run-down old ghost towns are great spots to hide for vagrants and outlaws who should be more scared of what's inside there than whatever it is they're running from on the outside."

Jacobi brought the shovel over, wondering why the tool was needed. Miller scooped nine shovels-worth of dirt from the middle of the crossroads.

While Twyla petted the necks of the eating horses, she asked, "Forgive the intrusion from someone so new to this partnership, but what are you doing—digging for gold?"

"Chuck's not here, where he last told Royce he'd be, so..." Miller grinded his teeth. "He's *forcing* me—*us*—to *summon* him..."

Twyla found that very odd.

"What, why?" Jacobi was confused.

"It's what he does, Jack." Miller grunted. "Otherwise, he wouldn't be able to call himself *The One and Only*, *Chuck Lafayette*, *Mythical Mystery Man,* or whatever he is, and all those other shid words that he's concocted."

"Oh," Jacobi responded. When he had met Charles Lafayette the second time, the magician had revealed the nature of the spectral encounter that had plunged him from his previous life into this new path in the West. Everything about Lafayette was indeed strange, secret, mysterious, shrouded...even terrifying...but the man did seem to know about things that most people would choose not to. "So, what's the hole for?"

Miller reached inside the chest of his rugged coat, unpinning an item. "We each need to sacrifice something of meaning to us." He placed a military medal—browned with age—into the hole. A clasp with a shield held a fabric ribbon of red, white and blue that held an eagle atop crossed cannons on cannonballs from which hung a five-pointed star containing an image of a shield-bearing robed woman defending against a crouching attacker.

"Surely you're not serious?" Twyla lit her fancy city lantern, helping to brighten the crossroads. "What manner of man would make such an...*occult*...request?"

"You should know, you've met him before." The veteran released a laboured sigh, having been in this situation with the magician many times himself."

"If I'm partaking of this *ritual*, I may as well start believing the tales of *spider-folk* in the mines of Boomtown."

"What's not to believe," Jacobi reasoned, "when you've seen the *ghost riders*..."

Twyla Matthias had to chew on that revelation for a moment. "Checkmate, Mister Nicholson, my king is defeated. Well played."

Jacobi admired the medallion resting in the crossroads hole, but didn't admire the disrespectful water starting to build up under it. "I never knew you had a medal. Is it from the war?"

Miller explained, "It's usually well-hidden. Thieves would love to get a hold of it." His thoughts rested for a few moments on his time in the Confederate Army, the senselessness of that slaughter, his eventual betrayal to the side of the Union, his time posted to the Takoda Indians and the irrationality and violence of their continual relocation. The man he had become since made better decisions, he hoped. He locked eyes with Jacobi. "I don't keep this because I am proud of it. I keep it as a reminder of what I did and didn't do right during the war."

Royce wiped rain from his nose. "You do alright in a pinch, old man."

Twyla put her lantern down. She unbuckled a saddlebag upon her horse, scooped a large handful of gold coins, and threw them into the shovelled hole.

"That won't do," Miller stated, flat.

"Not enough? It's valuable."

"Not valuable enough." Miller explained. "While all your coins and baubles have value, they're not valuable to you."

"Why not, gold was very dear to me?"

Miller explained further, "It's no sacrifice to a woman with so much."

"You're absolutely right." This is exactly what Twyla was learning upon this new path in life she had committed herself to. This *quest* to rescue Hawk.

This new quest to do better.

To *be* better.

She dug into another saddlebag and retrieved a round locket on a gold chain. "For many years, I forgot I even still had this." The reforming woman opened it, one side showing a small photograph of her younger self and the other a young man—they were both happy. She placed it within the hole next to Miller's medal. "This man was my Husband. His want for a simple rancher's life wasn't good enough for me, so I left him, and I soon had control of gold mines—even aetron. One day the Takoda attacked the ranch, he was all alone, and they killed him. I sold the land and never cared for Indians thereafter. This locket has now become a reminder to not follow that path."

"That sounds painful." Miller didn't know what else to say. "Jack?"

"I don't have anything that would count. I lost all I had on the *River Grace*. I now have some clothes, a hat, a gun and some friends."

Jacobi gave it some more thought. "Hawk gave me this strange trinket." He held it aloft, the lines of the remaining wood in the carving appearing like a spider's web in the lantern light.

"Did he tell you about it?" Miller asked.

"He said it had belonged to his brother—which is apparently you, Royce—and that I'd learn more when Fate and I found it necessary. Do you know more about it?"

Royce smiled. "I think he meant for you to discover most of that for yourself, Greenhorn."

Twyla liked that. "Sometimes we have to experience something for ourselves to fully understand its intrinsic value...just like seeing those ghost riders."

"You've come far, Jack." Miller smiled. "A lot of what Hawk says doesn't make sense at the time, but often leads to something when you least expect it. Stranger things like that are traces of the man he used to be before ending up with the likes of me. You know, we four wouldn't even be here, together, trying to find Lafayette, if not for your insistence to do something more drastic than just talking the ears off the Law. Twyla and I would probably still be arguing against those deaf ears in Sundown, to the point where they'd lock us both up for disturbing the peace."

Miller agreed with the item. "I say toss it in, Jack."

"Yes indeed," Twyla also agreed.

Jacobi wasn't sure. "What if Hawk wants it back, or, as I said, Royce it was apparently yours?"

"This is the West, Greenhorn." Royce took a step closer to Jacobi. "You can meet a man in a town and then never see him in that town ever again. Things are usually given for keeps. But, he gave that to you before he set out abruptly to scalp Twyla in Sundown."

Twyla's eyes lit with shocking memory.

"I'd assume, going into a white man's town as a red man to kill a prominent white woman, he wasn't expecting to be alive for long after," Miller explained. "I'd guess it's all part of that *Fate* that Lafayette harps on about. I don't try to understand it."

Jacobi thought about everything Hawk and Lafayette had told him. Instilled with the mysterious nature of his time in the West, he placed the charm necklace amongst the medal and the locket with coins.

"Your turn, Red." Miller nodded to Royce.

Jacobi was bewildered: Royce's hair was clearly as white as snow.

Royce scooped up the medal, locket, charm and coins as he removed his bowler hat. He placed the items inside like a bowl and placed the upside-down hat in the hole.

Jacobi found that a bit more respectful for the items as they rested inside Royce's hat.

"I'm going to regret this," Royce murmured.

There was no argument over using the hat and Miller had begun shovelling dirt back onto the hole before Royce's hand had been removed. The softened wet earth of the crossroads covered their items as the dirt went back in, Rusty inspecting the work with meticulous sniffing.

As Miller pressed on the mound of dirt with his boot to pat the soil down—Royce wincing in response as though he had just been shot in the heart—Jacobi asked, "Now what?"

Twyla was stroking the blaze of her horse. "Perhaps this mysterious showman wants us to cast a heathen *spell* of some sort?"

Royce laughed.

Miller groaned, "Don't joke, that's just the sort of thing he'd pull on us. Now we wait."

"For how long?" Jacobi asked.

"For as long as that fugging shyster wants to make us wait."

CHAPTER

TWENTY-ONE

They came under the cover of the storming darkness for their prisoner. A line of blue uniforms entered from one end of town down the main street, another line of blue uniforms coming from the other. These rows of soldiers, these columns of military men, marched with steadfast purpose.

The only helpful light in the dark of the storm was that cast by lanterns still managing to burn, swinging in the violent winds of the night.

The entire orchestration was overseen by the watcher of the storm. From behind the beaklike mask, the queues of soldiers were observed filing in. Black clad arms waved about in motion with the winds and rains, the dark clouds of the night obeying the watcher, dancing as one.

As the rain fell upon their blue caps, the soldiers merged with precision into the Sherrif's Office for their quarry—like blood into water. It was mere moments, and the soldiers were already leaving with their bound Indian prisoner.

This was as the watcher had predicted.
This was as the watcher had promised.

There were scarce few Sundown townsfolk that saw the transaction—those few that did viewed from behind gaps in shuttered windows.

Although surprised by the hour of their arrival, Sheriff Lahey simply stood back in what little room remained after unlocking Hawk's cell and receiving rain-soaked orders. He offered no resistance to allowing the custody of the prisoner to change hands. And he offered no objection to the violent way in which they moved the Indian.

The blue soldiers filed out in much the same manner they had entered. They were met by just as many more soldiers on horseback, each one of them bringing another man's horse.

With each soldier now on steed, the only person that remained on foot was the prisoner. The rain lashed at Hawk's bare shoulders, what was left of the painted bird and patterns on his body beginning to wash away.

The cavalry made its way out of town, the Indian prisoner's bound wrists tethered to one of the central soldier's horses.

Hawk turned around, walking backward so that he didn't lag, so he could see the mysterious watcher.

The watcher walked behind the cavalry, wiping the rain's spittle from the lenses of its corvid-beaked mask to better see the Indian prisoner.

CHAPTER

TWENTY-TWO

"This *Charles Lafayette*," Twyla adjusted a shawl over her outfit, her usual dresses were packed in the wagon and replaced by the shirt, pants and chaps of a cowboy, "is he often a rather trying individual?" She looked at her gold pocket watch, seeing that it was two minutes to midnight.

"You mustn't have spent long enough in his company." Miller went and stood beside the crossroads. His lantern was raised against the increasing rain of the storm.

"How *real* is this *summoning*?" Twyla asked. "It's all just tricks and bunkum with magicians, isn't it?"

"As strange as it sounds to the uninitiated, anything magical or mystical," Royce explained, "are the only things that seem real about our mysterious friend."

"How long will he make us wait?"

The question was answered by the gurgling croak of corvids all around.

Rusty's ears pricked and he barked with a defensive response. Jacobi eased him, stroking his fur, "Easy, Rusty."

Twyla kept the five horses calm, cooing.

"Ravens. Crows." Miller frowned. "Whatever they are."

Jacobi reiterated, "I said this place was creepy." He reached for his holstered gun, Twyla doing the same.

Royce chuckled. "Keep it together, Greenhorn."

Miller held out a hand for them to stop, explaining, "It's either every raven in Takoda Territory is here or it's one of Chuck's tricks." He asked Twyla, "What time is it?"

She raised an impeccable eyebrow. "I would like to say that it's *time for you to get a pocket watch*, but...it is coincidentally...just passing the stroke of...midnight."

"I bet it's Chuck." Miller shook his head. "Ravens and crows are like his symbol of magic or death or something."

"How theatrical," Twyla intoned.

"Exactly," Miller agreed. "But in case we get swarmed, keep a hand near your weapons."

Jacobi pointed, suddenly noticing that, "There's a light over there...coming from inside a...looks like, like, like a church—there wasn't any light shining over there earlier."

From inside one of the better-standing abandoned buildings of what was left of the town of Haven, a warm light was shining from inside boarded windows. The four travellers assured themselves that the light wasn't there during the waiting at the crossroads.

Armed with a lantern each and a hand near their firearms, leaving their horses behind, Jacobi, Miller, Royce and Twyla stepped carefully toward Haven. The croaking of surrounding corvids and the town's haunted reputation made them uneasy, including their dog following.

Twyla looked to Jacobi. "Are you travelling well?"

Jacobi swallowed. "I think I'd rather be over the edge of the *River Grace*."

"Well," Miller almost chuckled, "the Rubicon River isn't that far away, it's to our east."

Jacobi was shaking, quietly muttering, "Nope, nope, nope. Not helping at all..."

Rusty ran ahead, toward the light.

Jacobi swallowed his yell, "Rusty, back!"

The three had to step faster after the husky, their own rained-on illumination revealing the boarded-up church with rows of tombstones nearby among other broken buildings of the abandoned town.

The tombstones were many, their number disappearing into the edge of darkness that the lanterns couldn't shed light upon. Before any of the three could even read an epitaph, a familiar voice of showmanship from inside the church saved them the time.

"The Battle of Haven was a fortunate and unfortunate time for its residents during the Civil War. Those that died were spared the further horrors that followed; an unearthly disease and a native internment camp to name only a few."

"Chuck," Miller muttered under his breath.

Jacobi was the first to notice, "That entry was boarded up only moments ago…"

Sure enough, the entrance to the church was open to the world as though it had never been boarded closed. A single door still hung from a damaged hinge while light poured from inside.

As the four companions moved closer to the door, they recognised Charles Lafayette in his familiar magician's costume sitting at a round table with a soft green cover, four pews facing inward around it. They looked straight upon him, his calm black cat sitting beside.

Rusty—the animal no longer alert against the corvids—sat up on the pew to the magician's and feline's left, peering happily. The remaining two pews were empty, despite cards having been dealt on the table before the pew across from Lafayette. It appeared as though he and his cat were playing poker against an empty seat. At the centre of the table rested a familiar medal, locket, charm and hat—not a trace of rain, dirt or coins…or age.

Jacobi couldn't believe it as they all moved inside, dripping from the wet. The medal was clean and polished. The locket sparkled. The charm had no wear and tear. The hat was dried and brushed. Impossible!

"What the fugg, Chuck!" Miller was exasperated. "You could have just called us over."

"And deny you the sweet lullaby of a conspiracy of ravens, a murder of crows, a conventicle of corvids?"

"Are there birds out there or is it just you?"

Lafayette simply twizzled his moustache, a coy smile upon his un-answering face as the rain outside instantly became a downpour replacing the croaking corvids. "Just in a nick of time, I would say. That terrible storm is not meant for mortals to endure."

The rain beat down on the old boarded-up church, but not a drop fell through the roof to the hallowed ground.

Twyla stepped forward. "Excuse me, but those possessions are ours?" This was definitely the magician she and Jacobi played poker with on the *River Grace*.

"M'Lady Matthias, we meet again, if not for the first time or the last. You are, however, correct at this point in time, but moments ago those possessions were not yours."

"What are you suggesting?" Twyla was taken aback. "That locket has always been mine."

"The valiant Memphis, here," Charles leaned his head, the wide brim of his hat patting the back of the black cat's head, "just won your sacrificial effects back against all odds."

Jacobi swore the black cat looked proud of itself as its head was touched, if such a thing were possible. The bright yellow eyes even conveyed a certain level of smugness. He was afraid to ask, "From whom?"

"The lost souls of Haven, of course."

"Lost souls?" Jacobi just had to ask.

"Yes, M'Laddo. Don't you feel the hairs standing up on the back of your neck?" Charles grinned. "That's them…"

Because the sound of ravens had yielded to the howling storm, it enhanced Jacobi's fears as he sidestepped himself to look around for people that weren't there. "Well, I definitely do now!"

"If you're done with your pretentious show," Miller went for the empty pew across from Lafayette and Memphis, "we've come to talk." He sighed. "*We* want your help."

"Don't sit there!" Lafayette warned. "They don't like it when you sit *in* them. And...*pretentious?* One could take offence at such a description." The magician smirked. "I am, however, rather more impressed with the fact that you possess this modicum of such language. Miller, as they say in the saloons, my good company must be *rubbing off* on you."

"Unlikely," Miller rolled his eyes at the very thought as he sat next to Rusty while Jacobi and Twyla sat across from them. The pew across from Lafayette remained physically unoccupied as Royce just leaned behind it, placing his hands upon its backrest.

Miller breathed his frustration. "Can you help us. Hawk has been taken prisoner. Captain Cordell is about to resurface again. He's going to move Hawk via U.S. Army escort from Sundown to the Takoda Reservation, permanently."

"It's that last part we don't believe," Jacobi added.

"Jacobi Nicholson. M'Laddo...look at you." Charles Lafayette smiled. "You've gained yourself a splendid hat and spinning spurs, lost the fashionable clothes of Back East, and keep itching to reach for your shiny new revolver.

If I'm not mistaken, the man that Fate had fall from Grace to land in the West is becoming a real-life outlaw. Careful you don't fall too far...*Jack*..."

"Well..." Jacobi didn't know how to respond. "Why did you call...how did you know Miller calls me *Jack*?"

"Are you willing to shoot a man with that?" The magician glanced to Jacobi's gun belt.

"If I have to...to free Hawk, I would."

"You have changed, indeed, M'Laddo." The magician thought a moment. "*Jack the Outlaw*, if you want my help," Charles Lafayette began returning the sacrificial items, their owners amazed at their like-new condition, "I need to know that you are willing to do what it takes. This will be a battle, not just a duel between two desperados in the street. Your mortality is at stake. One of us, all of us, may die—we may fail. Souls will rise and souls will burn. Just make sure that if you weave Fate—if you spin Wyrd—you are ready to spin it beyond the consequences."

There was a certain realisation around the poker table in the crumbling church at Haven. This had become very real. What they were planning was outright against the law of the land and involved mortal danger. Their very lives hung in the balance.

The magician continued. "You know what unites us, but you barely speak of it, as though you would be considered insane, even among those that have shared the same ethereal experience. Fate has chosen to unite us, all in a different manner, by our visions of the ghost riders."

Twyla tested her scepticism of the magician. "How would you even know what we have seen?"

Miller rolled his eyes. "Don't ask."

"You've seen them too?" Jacobi asked, looking from Miller to Royce to the magician. He sensed that Lafayette must have seen them, whether that was how he gained his esoteric knowledge about them or not, but he never told of it when they met—and Miller was just the sort of man that would keep such things tightly locked until he knew you well enough. And Royce...well, Royce liked to talk, but Royce was mostly a closed book.

"More times than you could fathom, M'Laddo," Charles bowed his brimmed head.

"My dreams, both waking and not, would be the fabric of your nightmares."

The magician raised his head. "But, did you know, one among us has not witnessed the ghost riders for their self? Would that change your view of what unites us?"

"Who cares?" Royce said, flat.

Jacobi asked, "Who hasn't?"

"Me, Greenhorn." Royce answered. "I haven't." Jacobi watched Royce put his bowler hat back upon his head, crushing the white mane of hair under it.

"You haven't?" Jacobi was stunned. He had assumed Royce had seen them somewhere in his past, because he so readily believed Jacobi's story of the ghost riders without hesitation. He'd had no objections against Hawk sending him and Miller to make introductions with Lafayette. "So, what does that mean?"

"It doesn't change anything," Royce answered. "I've seen some fugging strange shid in my time, let me tell you, and I believe that you all have seen the ghost riders, and that's all that's ever mattered to me—it has always been enough for me."

Twyla agreed, "I concur. It shouldn't change anything."

"Maybe," Royce added, "I've got my internal compass squared away, or more likely I'm just not as unlucky as you lot."

Jacobi spoke directly to Lafayette. "What we have or haven't seen is not at stake here. Hawk's life is. We're all united by this phenomenon whether we've seen it or not. Royce is still one of those who will try to free Hawk, ghost riders witness or not. What better reason is there to unite than simply to free a man that will be murdered for being a product of trying to live by the way of his people as a world he didn't ask for continued to force his Fate in this...this *West*, this *Wyrd* West. As strange as it is, we who have seen the ghost riders or not have been brought together around Hawk's particular Fate."

With a proud smile, Lafayette asked Jacobi, "Do you sense something in Hawk's Fate?"

"When we met, you offered your services on a condition." Jacobi held aloft the charm of the feather-adorned necklace. "I feel that Hawk's Fate is headed towards that condition." Jacobi brought forth an aspect of his deep conversation with the magician. "I feel that Hawk's Fate is converging to the point of Doom..."

The magician nodded. "Thus is Fate."

"Thus is Fate," Jacobi added, feeling as though he finally understood the phrase.

PART VI

CROSSING THE RUBICON

CHAPTER

TWENTY-THREE

The timing was perfect for Captain Phileas Cordell of the United States Army. The prisoner transfer was of his own meticulous design. It was not created to obey the laws of any man, but instead higher powers that most could not understand or dare to comprehend.

Higher powers that he continued to gain favour with.

The protocol established between the Sundown Sheriff's Office and the La Grande Bureau of Indian Affairs was but a trifle detail in the captain's scheme. Those institutes wanted the prisoner escorted from Sundown by armed guard to keep the townsfolk calm. Going to Fort Morgan in the East to acquire more soldiers to help protect the transfer for when the procession went north-west was Cordell's contribution. It would then travel to the Takoda Reservation to deliver the prisoner.

Those few loyal to Cordell's extreme sense of defeating the Indians in the West at all costs understood that their prisoner would not survive the night inside Fort Morgan. It was very easy to kill a prisoner and stage the incident as a failed attempt at escape.

Those fewer in number loyal to Cordell by powers from beyond this world understood that the prisoner would never reach Fort Morgan, but instead was doomed to die to those higher powers.

Phileas Cordell rode at the head of the two by ten long procession of cavalry, followed by ten horse-drawn wagons filled with sitting infantry. His beaten Indian prisoner had suffered the torrential rain but now suffered the blazing sun as he tried to keep pace on foot, wrists bound and tethered to one of the rear cavalry horses. The prisoner hadn't even been brought before Cordell, just simply dragged, stumbling behind.

LUKE TRACEY

Among the army's number were two individuals that did not belong to any official military service.

Unofficially? Well, that was different.

Victor Quartus Falco hadn't appreciated the stormy weather. He had to shut down the zapping electrical contraptions strapped to his body, each gizmo potentially a danger around water. He wasn't accustomed to marching. Thankfully, his frail frame didn't have to bear the weight of his devices alone. The horse he was assigned didn't seem to like him very much and unlike the other horses, this one didn't seem to be very good at obeying commands. He had tried to catch up to the mysterious figure in front of him, the one that Captain Cordell seemed to favour over his army men, but the figure either simply didn't hear him under the mask or—as is often the case with Victor—he was ignored.

The masked figure rode in solitude, making no conversation with the military. Cordell would constantly look back to check on the wearer of the black-clad bird-mask, and the figure was always checking on where the Indian prisoner was at. There was a sense of fear around the dark figure, as such agents were known to operate in important campaigns across the United States of America with great authority.

No soldier questioned the presence of these two strangers, even as mysterious as they were. Such were the constant dealings and plans of their captain.

Passing the Takoda Oil Fields, named because it was where a group of Takoda Indians had been forcibly removed years earlier—although history often omits that fact—filled Captain Cordell with a sense of pride and power.

East of Sundown, north of Mudflats, west of Rubicon River, the smokestacks belched their black plumes. The thick smoke was accompanied by the industrious wrenching and clanging of oil being drawn from the earth.

The oil fields were one of the biggest signs that the modernising industrial world of Back East was intruding into the wild frontiers of the West.

The Captain could have simply put his two guests and most of—if not all of—his men on board a train from Sundown through the Takoda Oil Fields toward and over the

Rubicon eastward. But Cordell wasn't going to afford the luxury of modern transport to his Indian prisoner. As far as he was concerned, Cordell was forcing the last rebellious Indian of the Haven Indian Internment Camp massacre to be confronted by the progress of civilisation. A progress made possible since forcing his people to scatter from this land.

Now all that remained for Cordell was the final plan for this Indian.

CHAPTER

TWENTY-FOUR

The weather was much better and during the quiet moments Twyla Matthias would occasionally insert a spark of words to ignite a conversation during the journey.

It turns out she was more than just an obsession with gold and fashion.

"Have either of you three ever heard of the term, *Deus ex Machina?*"

She did worry that Miller either was not interested in anything she had to say or much of her conversations were beyond his comprehension—or that he really did hate her.

Miller rode shotgun, looking back over the sight of supply crates, weapons and ammunition that had mysteriously appeared in their wagon after meeting with Lafayette. Twyla rode her horse beside their two-horse wagon, Jacobi at the reigns, Hawk's horse tethered behind. The red husky explored the trail ahead with reckless abandon, trying to keep up with Royce and his horse.

Still developing his skill driving the two-horse wagon, Jacobi found the course that had been laid out for them from the ruins of Haven to the dreaded Fort Morgan to be increasingly difficult. But according to Lafayette, it would *cause as little vibration in the Web of Fate as possible to avoid detection until the time of opportunity presented itself.*

"So, what is a..." Jacobi wondered, "*day-us-ecks-mack-in-uh* or whatever you called it?"

"*Deus ex Machina.*" Twyla began, delighted for the opportunity to have an educated conversation. "It began centuries ago, used in theatrical performances."

Miller snorted. "Sounds like something Lafayette would like to hear about if he were here."

"Indeed," Twyla agreed, adjusting her gold-rimmed spectacles. "It was a device used by storytellers to often solve a narrative, by inserting a divine character, such as a god, to fix everything: *magic-poof-solved*. The machine was the device that lowered the divine being onto the stage. It sometimes went against any logic built during the story, robbing the audience of everything they had learned to believe or disbelieve so far. But what I find most interesting, just lately in my life, is the term translated—it means, *God from the Machine*.

Jacobi asked the question that Miller was thinking. "Why does that catch your attention?"

"Imagine, Gentlemen, if you will, the world as a stage—a machine—and we are the characters. Events have weaved our destinies together, like we are all trains on separate tracks that are merging into each other."

Jacobi raised the charm from his chest, Miller also seeing it. The two of them understood that something unknown was at work, from Hawk to Lafayette, to Twyla's own words. Fate was leading them all somewhere.

"During this," Twyla continued, "against our understanding of all that we knew before, enters that which removes all we previously understood of our own narratives…"

Jacobi and Miller looked at each other, admitting together out loud what Lafayette had made them realise that they didn't speak enough of for fear of being considered insane: "the ghost riders..."

Pleased, she tipped her rancher's hat. "Exactly. And speaking of subjects that we don't broach often," Twyla inquired, "it would appear that you have seen ghost riders yourself, Miller, but I have not had the pleasure of hearing the tale...unless, of course, it is a private matter?"

As Jacobi guided the horses, he looked straight at the side of Miller's weathered face. "Neither have I..."

"It's never really come up, and I would have eventually told young Jack here the story, but I have no worries telling it to you both now."

Miller began.

"You know I fought in the *War Between the States*—our *Civil War*. I was conscripted into the Confederate Army, forced to fight for something that I didn't believe in. I was taken prisoner, easily—as I couldn't bring myself to shoot to actually kill a North soldier—and then swore allegiance to the Union Army. I became what they called a *galvanised yankee*. From then on, I fought for the North on the Western Frontier, away from any real battles between the States."

The man swallowed, stroking his beard. "I was placed under the command of the infamous *Captain Phileas Cordell*. Like most Union soldiers, the man didn't trust ex-Confederates. And even though he was a Union man, he would often express to us that *we had failed the cause*, as though he had interest in the Confederate states winning." Miller shook his head with unpleasing memories.

"He especially didn't like people like me who didn't blend into his army's culture of superiority. He was so against anyone that didn't have white skin or fit his idea of a *true* American. He never really fought to free slaves and his campaigns were mostly directed against what was referred to as the *Indian Problem*. He always claimed to be fighting for a higher purpose and hoped the war between North and South continued as it gave him the ability to fight on the Western Frontier without much oversight from superiors."

"I'm now sorry to have known and dealt with the man," Twyla interjected, "but you saw a side of Cordell that I only saw the surface of. I knew he wasn't right in the head, and sadly that was to my advantage."

"I always thought that he was sick in the head," Miller added, "like he just enjoyed the killing and didn't want it to stop. But there was something deeper in him, a grand design to everything he did."

"How did you fit into it all?" Jacobi asked.

"I really didn't," Miller answered. "Eventually, to get rid of me, he assigned me to the relocation of the last groups of Takoda Indians to the Reservation that had been made for them."

Jacobi watched Miller's eyes lower with melancholic memory. "I could tell you everything that went wrong, but you'd be listening for days, so for the matter of the ghost riders, it begins and ends with a young girl, not even ten years old. In our language, her name was, *Little Flower*. She had been given a puppy by the name of *Rusty*."

Miller caught Jacobi's surprised glance. "That's right, Jack. Our Rusty, when he was nothing more than a ball of red fluff, was given to Little Flower by Hawk's half-brother—that loser you know currently scouting ahead. Royce has always loved animals."

"So, if they're half-brothers, Royce and Hawk," Jacobi asked, "which parent do they share?"

"Well, the bounty posters never let Royce forget his father or the family that came with that. Always had him listed as *Royce 'Red Roy' Falco*. They shared the same mother, an Indian woman. I bet you've probably heard of Royce's father: *Oskar Falco*—the big time German railroader."

Jacobi nodded, the name was known Back East.

"I knew Oskar Falco," Twyla admitted.

"Of course you did," Miller sighed.

"Oh?" Jacobi listened intently, looking ahead to Rusty as he ran circles around Royce's horse. The red husky carried his own history. He had watched the dog assume it was leading the wagon as it found countless things to sniff along the way.

"Little Flower had lost her parents to bandits," Miller continued. "The remaining

Takoda continued to raise her; especially Hawk."

"Our Hawk?" Jacobi asked, as Twyla dealt with inner turmoil arising from newer parts of a story that she knew that she was responsible for.

"The same." Miller remembered. "In those days, he was known as *Red Hawk*—*red* like his brother. He had lost many people that were close to him—some very close. Lost to the War Between the States that his people had nothing to do with, to settlers going West, to bandits, to relocation. But he wasn't broken by any of it...yet."

Twyla dabbed her eyes with the kerchief that hung around her neck.

"He had a rebellious fire, but he was a very spiritual man. All his life, Hawk had visions of a Thunderbeing that kept his spirit sturdy."

Jacobi had to interrupt. "When I saw the ghost riders, I saw Hawk among them, riding a giant bird that was shooting lightning!"

"Why do you think he had me take you to see Chuck the showman?" Miller smiled at Jacobi before elaborating. "All his life, he dreamed that a giant bird was flying toward him, its wings beating with the sound of thunder, and lightning shooting from its eyes. Apparently, it's what was painted on his chest," Miller glanced at Twyla, "before he went for your scalp."

Twyla passed a hand over the area.

"Such visions of a Thunderbird among the Takoda led him to become a *Spiritwalker*...it's like a medicine man or a holy man."

Jacobi added, "A *shaman*."

"That's right," Miller nodded. "So Red Hawk led his group in a sort of," Miller tried to conjure the right words, "*spiritual* resistance. They were a group of families in continued defiance of the white man, planting their *tipis* away from the lands they had lost but not going to the reservation. How could they go wrong when they had a Spiritwalker among them? The Horse Nation even started to call him *Thunder Hawk,* in honour of the Thunderbird he embodied."

Miller's head bowed. "But, soon enough, the white man wanted to mine for gold, oil and that blasted aetron on their very camp. I continued to do my duty. I had become friendly, I negotiated Indian Officers visiting, I tried to convince the Takoda to comply, to do what was in their best interest. But it was the same story, over and over for them, time and again: *that piece of land you're on, you must move, we want it.* And when they didn't move, that's when the army came...and I didn't fight for either side...I remember Royce was visiting and he fought, like a firecracker, covered in the blood of soldiers, while I didn't."

"I sadly remember that day." Twyla Matthias took a turn to bow her head. "They came with Captain Cordell at their head, my disgraceful self not far behind. I may as well have paved the way with bricks of gold, for that is what I paid Captain Cordell and his loyal soldiers to get the job done by any means necessary. Today I am ashamed, that path of gold leading to the Indian camp became stained with blood. The Takoda fought back with *Thunder* Hawk: guns, bows, axes, their bare hands, on foot, on horseback...it was no use, though—half of them were slaughtered."

Miller's eyes welled. "There's an abandoned mine there, still to this day."

"There was nothing in the land for the greed of men," Twyla added. "No gold. No oil. No aetron. I even sold the mine to a desperate settler afterwards for more than it would have been worth." Twyla had to clean the fog from her spectacles. "Where were they taken, Alfred?"

Miller hated his first name being used, but he and Twyla both didn't even realise that it had.

"Haven. An Indian internment camp was set up in the ruins of the town."

"Haven?" Jacobi was connecting histories. "The camp that Lafayette mentioned?"

"There's a thousand terrible things that have happened in Haven since it was founded," Miller answered. "It wasn't important enough at the time to explain further, and that place already had you shaking in your little cowboy boots."

Jacobi agreed. He wondered about that accursed town of Haven. *How could such a place be the site of so many terrible things.*

"Royce was tried and convicted. He was a real outlaw, a real fugging Wild West gunslinger, with countless bounties on his head as well as having just fought the US Army. His connected father managed to make sure that he only saw the inside of a prison for a short time rather than the gallows. And you know what, that's Royce's problem in life; he's so impulsive and thinks he's invincible and can escape consequences. He thinks that no gallows will have him, or any prison will hold him. He'll think that way until his luck runs out and he does find himself at the end of a noose." Miller shook his head.

"Anyway...what was I saying? Ah, yeah. Cordell didn't have me discharged for trying to keep the peace during the battle, instead assigning me to oversee the rehabilitation of the Takoda. Let me tell you both, it was more of a punishment than being discharged and he knew I would feel it that way. His entire method of command seemed based on causing the most misery to others. I regret every day of overseeing the rehabilitation. They assimilated them, especially the children, cutting their hair, forbidding them to speak their own language, and forcing them to take American names. It was Hell on Earth. Many died from starvation, being overworked, no heat. The only saving grace, if it can be called that despite all the other afflictions, was that disease hadn't become a problem."

It was Miller's turn to wipe his eyes, his sleeve passing over his face. "This absolute horror continued until Little Flower died, Rusty howling to the sky in her lifeless arms. Something had been dying in Thunder Hawk since his imprisonment and it finally died with Little Flower. That something in his eyes—the Thunderbird and the Spiritwalker—both gone, replaced by a spirit of vengeance."

"I've seen those eyes." Twyla passed her fingers again over her tomahawk wound, seeing that Miller understood.

"As I stared upon those Takoda that remained, Thunder Hawk's fists curled, and the sky...I don't know how to describe it other than...it opened up, a storm bursting upon the ruins of Haven and especially upon the internment camp." Miller caught his breath as he finally reached the further unbelievable part of his story. "To this day, it still chills me to my bones. *They*, still chill me to my bones. There are those that saw nothing amiss. But I tell you, I did, I saw them, I saw a great host of them. They just appeared, ghostly horseman, riders on the storm, herding fiery cattle among black birds. They descended upon the internment camp as the Indians began to revolt."

There was a pause that Jacobi needed to end. "What happened next?"

"One of the riders flew by, as if he knew me, he called to me, *Alfred, Alfred Miller.* Nobody calls me *Alfred*. He told me to finally do what was right or join them herding their hellish stampede forevermore. I had a standard issue rifle in my hand and a crossroads of a decision in my head. Serving my country and serving the Takoda were not the same—I needed to choose which was right."

The seconds that Jacobi and Twyla waited for Miller to continue felt like years.

"I said fuggoff to the army. I killed my first soldier that day, and not the last. By the time Thunder Hawk and I were done, the ghost riders had gone and the internment camp at Haven was more of a burned husk of bad memories. Not one soldier lived to tell the tale that I had turned against them."

Miller took a second to breathe.

"Thunder Hawk and I escaped the area, taking the remaining Takoda—the living and the dead—to their Reservation. Fate, Thunder Hawk said, no matter how much they tried to resist, was dooming the Takoda and the rest of the Horse Nation to life on reservations. But, Thunder Hawk refused to live there, vowing that he couldn't rest until Twyla Matthias and Phileas Cordell paid for their crimes—even if it took years. He rode back into the plains of his people, continuing to raise Rusty, never forgetting what happened. Since that day, he tells me that he has not seen his thundering spiritbird again, and dropped that part of his name, becoming simply *Hawk*—or Red Hawk as known to the white man—like I told you, they finally killed something in his very spirit that day, and it has never returned. I, hopefully, would be presumed dead as no soldiers survived the battle at the camp. I now live with the land, a trapper and hunter, only using my time in that Civil War when it offers an advantage in lawful society. Hawk and Royce and I would often meet, as little as days or as long as months apart, Rusty often our line of communication. Hawk never doubted my seeing the ghost riders, nor I him, and because of those spirits we made a different life apart from the world of civilisation that keeps coming West."

Miller finished. "Things had been this way until you, Jack, fell from a boat and into our lives, having also seen the ghost riders."

CHAPTER

TWENTY-FIVE

"There it is, Jack, in all its glory," Miller declared, passing his worn binoculars to Jacobi so that he could also get a better look. *"Rubicon Crossing."*

Twyla looked through her own brass-rimmed binoculars. "That magnificent bridge is sometimes considered to be the point of no return, connecting the civilised *modernity* of the East to the wild *frontier* of the West." She was glad to be almost resting after days of following Lafayette's mysterious directions through some rugged trackless regions. "It gets its name from the fact that the locals call this river the *Rubicon* rather than the *Missouri* as it appears on maps."

THUNDER ROAD

Jacobi gazed at the massive metal truss bridge through the binoculars. Steel arches and beams appeared like a silver web of perfected industry. It stretched from a cliff edge in the East, spanning incredibly high over the southward rushing waters of the enormous Missouri River to meet another cliff edge in the West. Rubicon Crossing was a marvel of American civilisation and engineering, allowing movement into the West by road and rail. "Coming from Boston, I thought I had seen it all. The frontier continues to impress me."

Jacobi couldn't help but notice that the bridge's design was oddly reminiscent of the charm that Hawk had given him and that a few ravens were perched atop the structure.

Three ravens, to be exact.

"Gentlemen," Twyla politely interrupted, "I think it's about to become much more impressive..."

Miller grabbed his binoculars back from Jacobi with a brisk jerk, looking to where Twyla spoke of. To the west of the bridge approached a procession of blue-uniformed soldiers riding on the wooden plank road that was beside the railroad track.

"That's gotta be Cordell at the lead with the captain's rank," Miller stated, having not seen the man in years. "None of the horses are branded, though, they're not U.S. Army property."

Twyla had been studying the leader also, the captain sitting atop a healthy steel-grey horse, her memory of a fruitful partnership now filled her with revulsion. It was a sudden change, but seeing the ghost riders while having a tomahawk blade at your scalp can do that to a person. "He often spoke of a *Higher Power*, that *America's Manifest Destiny and the gods of the white, black, brown, yellow and red were just pawns in a cause that dwindled in comparison*. He knew people in high places, that I could be sure of, but there was always something sinister—something hidden—about this Higher Power. He did unusual, peculiar things, disappearing at night, absent on long journeys, able to call in favours from unexpected places, avoiding where possible anything that registered his name. These horses, for example, would have been bought with blood money away from the records of the army. His way of keeping some of the extent of his force unregistered. It keeps whatever his clandestine activities are unknown. But, with regards to his identity, I can vouch that that lily-looking officer is definitely Cordell."

"I'll give you a clue." Royce was kneeling next to Rusty, the length of a spyglass extended toward the same man being discussed. "*Sicarius*. That's what he's a part of. That's what they call themselves: the *Sicarius Assembly*. Made up of a shadowy few, but their reach bigger than we could imagine."

Twyla looked to Royce. "How do you know of such things?"

"Lady," Royce smiled, "the things I know would pop you right outta your skin."

Miller handed his binoculars back to Jacobi, the young man chortling, "Look at him. What's with the lady's hair?" He quickly realised what he had said, looking to Twyla and her bun of brunette hair behind a rancher's hat with apology, the usually long hair bound instead for travelling in the wild. "Sorry."

"Not at all," Twyla smirked. "It's how we of the more *upper-crust* of society flaunt ourselves. Why some men, like Cordell, had to take it that step further, I'll never understand."

Cordell brushed his long curling spirals of blonde hair over his shoulder with a gloved hand, then pressed his thick moustache flatter to his face. He was king of an almost-rogue group of soldiers with the frontier of the West as theirs for the taking.

"There's Hawk!" Miller spotted the Indian prisoner among the cavalry. "We can't even try here. There's so many soldiers that there won't be any room for him to move on the bridge. We'll have to wait until they've crossed it, follow ourselves, and prepare an ambush.

"Fugginell." Royce lowered his spyglass, mouth agape. "What's Victor got himself involved in now?"

"Hey?" Miller asked.

"Victor's with them, like Twyla said back in Sundown. He's wearing some sort of electric contraption."

Jacobi had taken the binoculars from Miller. "He's a gizmologist…seen a few Back East."

Royce nodded. "You got that right, Greenhorn. He's always been like some sort of mad scientist with all the things he's invented.

Victor's been almost blowing himself up since the day he was born. That includes the Falco mansion where we grew up in La Grande."

Jacobi inhaled a short breath. "What's that—the masked rider?"

Twyla had eyes on the same person. "That's a plague doctor. An agent of the government sent to investigate and prevent the spread of disease."

Miller inserted, "They became a prominent force because of the disease caused by the so-called *Indian Problem*. They get a lot of freedom to interfere where they like."

Twyla agreed. "They're outfits are supposed to protect them from sickness. Cordell often uses them when dealing with Indians."

"That's bullshid." Royce dropped his spyglass. "Plague doctors, they're just inquisitors of Sicarius. They're bad news. They know how to spin Wyrd the wrong way. They're not weavers of Fate; their reavers."

Jacobi was still alarmed by the black rider's presence. "Doesn't anyone else see the black cloud hanging around that plague doctor?"

Royce had his spyglass back over his eye in his left hand while his right hand single-handedly shuffled some cards and then made them simply disappear. "Our Greenhorn's right. I can see it now. You've got some natural talent, kid."

Almost dancing around the spectacled beaked mask of the Plague Doctor shifted a translucent black cloud. Jacobi had seen this phenomenon before. "That's the same black mist that surrounds a..."

"*Trikuhl*," Royce breathed.

Miller placed his hand upon his face like he had a headache. "Soldiers. Cordell. Gizmologist. Reaver. Trikuhl. How deep in the shid have we got ourselves this time?"

The beaten Hawk, wrists glistening red from the rope that bound him, was led like one of the horses before Captain Cordell. Hawk finally saw, face-to-face, the one responsible for commanding so much of the destruction upon the spirit of his people.

Phileas Cordell ignored the prisoner, barking orders. "Send a scout, reconnoitre farther along the tracks eastward, make sure a train is not coming this way. I don't want civilian eyes anywhere near this area. Watch the northern and southern trails at either end. I don't want any mountain men or this prairie worshipper's tribes," he now regarded Hawk, "coming this way. Nobody is to get through here until we are clear of the bridge."

The soldiers complied, scurrying about. The cavalry entered first, Cordell at their lead with the horse with the prisoner now beside him. The wagons, with their crates of ammunition, provisions and other camp supplies, each waited their turn to enter the bridge single-file beside the railroad tracks.

Captain Cordell checked his pocket watch, then addressed the prisoner for the first time with enough pompous volume that many of his soldiers could also hear. "I'm not going to even dignify you with an attempt at pronouncing the name you refused to give up. The orders, though, officially state your name as *Red Hawk*, but that just has to be some translation of your prairie critter-speak."

Hawk kept stepping with the pace of the horse he was bound to, eyes remaining lowered to the bridge.

"What was the name given to you at the Haven Indian Internment Camp?"

Hawk remained solemn, unyielding.

Cordell waved a gloved finger.

A soldier struck the Indian across the face with the butt of a rifle.

"Again," Cordell asked, "what was the name they gave you at the Haven Indian Internment Camp? And remember, we speak *American* here."

Hawk looked up at Cordell, the Captain's face bringing years of pain back to his mind. But he walked with defiance against the question.

A scout returned, saluting, delivering news. "Captain. No sign of approaching trains ahead."

"Excellent." Cordell didn't return the salute. "Join the ranks."

As the scout fell in line with the cavalry, the captain's attention reverted to the Indian. "Still, no answer?"

Cordell turned to his closest soldier as they slowly rode. "Give me your service revolver."

Without hesitation, the soldier handed his superior the weapon.

Cordell emptied the chambers, the rounds falling to the tracks. He held the weapon to Hawk. "Take this."

Cordell could see there was going to be no compliance. The captain kicked Hawk in the gut.

While the Indian was curled over, Cordell dismounted, holding the procession that had wholly made it on to the bridge.

He thrust the revolver into the waist of Hawk's buckskin pants and cut his ropes free with an exotic, jagged knife. The blade was formed of a strange silver weave. "Now, *savage*, march ahead..." He turned to some of his soldiers. "Remain here. If he runs away from me, shoot him in the leg."

Jacobi wanted to know, "Why is Hawk just taking this?"

"There's got to be well-more than fifty soldiers about," Miller answered. "There's not much he can do."

"Yeah," Jacobi nervously agreed, "but if we also don't do anything, it may end up being too late. I've only learned guns recently, but I know what itchy trigger fingers are—and I've got itchy trigger fingers right now."

"As cryptic as his small number of details were when Jacobi managed to get him to help us," Royce reminded, "one of the last things Lafayette said to us was to *wait for a sign.*"

Miller answered, "Whilst I find the antics of Chuck Lafayette fugging infuriating, the man has a mysterious way of providing what we have needed at the right times. I have never felt more ridiculous wearing these belts of ammunition or switching to those bullets with Lafayette's strange mystical symbols etched on them. I mean, what is the bullet made of, aetron? But, I'm sure the magician has provided them for another of his inexplicable setups that I am assuming will pay off again and leave me fugging dumbfounded."

"It better happen soon, we're running out of time." Jacobi didn't mind the ammunition belts, or the extra guns and cartridges—all of which had mysteriously appeared in their wagon after enlisting the assistance of the magician. The symbol etched upon each of Lafayette's bullets was the same as Jacobi's charm.

The four of them looked armed and dangerous, ready for anything. The matter now, was the timing of when to strike to free Hawk. Over fifty soldiers and their unexpected allies versus four very-to-be-outlaws of the West.

Jacobi wondered if they were going to succeed or be shot down in a blaze of glory. "I still don't get why Hawk isn't doing anything. Is he waiting for Fate to doom him or something?"

As Hawk was walking over Rubicon Crossing, from farther eastward came a metallic squeal.

A small black railcar rolled along swiftly.

Soldiers armed their rifles while Cordell kept his knife ready for potential danger, barking, "I thought you said there weren't any trains coming?"

The scout was pale. "There weren't any, Captain, I assure you."

"I don't believe it..." Miller gave the binoculars to Jacobi. "Other side of the bridge. Is *this* the fugging sign?"

Twyla answered Jacobi's question of "What?" with "It's Charles Lafayette!"

Sure enough, standing atop his wagon of black with gold decoration, as it coasted slower along the rails, was a man decked out in a lavish tailored midnight blue suit. His showy caravan may have traded wagon wheels for those used by trains, but it still showed no signs of how it was actually propelled.

No horses. No pumping mechanisms. No steam boiler. The thing just rolled along.

The caravan came to a perfect stop on its unconventional train wheels. The new arrival pulled out a handheld cone and raised the smaller end to his moustached lips under his overly-wide-brimmed hat. "Step right up, folks, come one, come all," the magician began, booming louder beyond what could be expected of the cone, "let me introduce myself..."

CHAPTER

TWENTY-SIX

Captain Cordell waved—annoyed—for the magician's attention. "Pardon me. You'll need to move from the tracks. Take your," he couldn't see how the thing moved, "train, and go back the way you came immediately or be charged with treason. This here is an enterprise of the United States Army."

Lafayette removed the cone away from his mouth. "Never interrupt the man with the speaking-trumpet or the show won't go on!"

Putting the device back to his lips while climbing down from his caravan one-handed, the broadcast continued. "I am the One and Only, Charles Lafayette, Illusionist, Magician, Perceptivist, Master of Cosmology, Esoterica,

Fortuna, Portentia and Mysticism, Purveyor or the Wyrd and Wonderful." He turned and bowed when he reached the bottom. "At your service." The magician tilted his wide hat and struck a proud legs-parted arms-crossed chin-raised pose before the army captain's eyes.

Cordell pointed his knife, to which the magician remarked of the blade: "A silk weave spun by unseen folk that move among the cobwebs?"

"You wouldn't know of such things. The threat of treason will be raised to death if you don't back away now." Cordell looked over the magician's face. "I'm not usually in the habit of giving your kind second chances, so I suggest you get on board your little train-thing and remove yourself from my sight."

Lafayette ignored the veiled racial insult with the practiced grace of an actor, lowering the cone and raising an eyebrow. "My *kind*...do you have something against *magicians*? Forgive me, Captain, but you don't know what I've come to know. From spiders to nightmares. I do not fear death. Although, you and I must catch that particular train one day. Speaking of which: you may want to miss the next train."

"Next train?" Cordell was losing his patience, becoming befuddled by the magician.

Lafayette caught sight of Hawk. "Well...that Indian you have there, M'Captain, I believe I know him."

The Captain edged his weapon closer to Lafayette's face. "Do you now?"

"Yes indeed," Lafayette continued, the speaking-trumpet sliding the knife away as it returned to his mouth. "I do apologise as his name has slipped my mind." All the soldiers were paying attention, including the sparking gizmologist and the shadowy plague doctor. "Thundering Storm? Or something. Storm Dog. Storm Mongrel. Or was it, Windy Something? Perhaps, Windy Pooch. Windy Mutt. Or Breezy Badger. No, perhaps Pink Elephant, or something else. You know well, Captain, these *prairie-dog-types*, it's so difficult to keep up with their naming conventions."

Lafayette locked eyes with the Falco brother, almost admiring the suit of electrical conduction he wore. There was no recognition from behind Victor's smudged goggles, and that's the way the magician wanted it.

The plague doctor, well Charles knew that was going to be a different story...

"If you are in collusion with this savage, you'll be treated just as he is," Cordell barked.

"Look at how he just stands there," the magician shook his head, ignoring the captain's words, "tempting *Fate*..."

Jacobi swore that Lafayette looked right at him through the binoculars for the briefest second.

"Reminds me of the time I once saw— *Thunder Hawk!*—yes, that is his name, I knew it would come back to me." Lafayette applied the pressure of his showmanship. "Anyway, I once saw this particular prairie-man stand up to a bear. It was roaring at him, growling, spittle dripping from its face, claws ready to rip him to shreds. The fool just stood there, locking eyes with the beast."

"Put the cone down! Is there a point to your constant incessant *yammering*?" Cordell's tolerance for civility had faded.

"There is. I implore your patience for just a moment longer. *So*, the bear didn't really calm down, but it did turn around and crawl away while having a raging fit—a complete conniption! Thunder Hawk just stood there, as if he assumed the big ugly beast wouldn't kill him by simply losing interest and walking away. Well, Captain, he was right."

Jacobi looked to Miller. "Did he...did...did Lafayette just tell us why Hawk is just standing there...with a story about a bear? Like, that the bear is Cordell and he'll just go away? Or is it that he *won't* go away like the bear?"

"Maybe, maybe not." Miller frowned. "But that busdud is using one of my stories. Chuck never saw Hawk stand up to a bear—I did! *That's. My. Story.* I was there; not him. The fugging busdud!"

Twyla frowned. "I do indeed hope then that the bear story is not the sign we are waiting on...?"

Captain Cordell shook his knife before Lafayette's face, sensing a degree of cunning, that this magician may actually possess knowledge beyond most others.

Like those of the Sicarius Assembly.

Perhaps he should ask the plague doctor. "That's it. Both of you, kneel, hands behind your head." No, he wouldn't ask the plague doctor.

"Fugg. We're too late," Miller stood up, ready to run in as Hawk and Lafayette obeyed.

Jacobi, before coming to the West, never would have trusted or believed in such a thing as Fate. He barely had the tolerance for the religious practices of his adopting family. He held the charm around his neck, waiting for a sign—somehow knowing—and raised a finger for his companions to, "Wait..."

"Fate has been kind," the captain stated. "There will be two sacrifices instead of one." Cordell looked to the mask of the plague doctor and all about, as though he had a grander audience than the sizeable one collected around him. "*Qonkura* will be pleased." He commanded, "Fetch the sacraments. We're doing the ritual now."

The plague doctor dismounted.

"But, Captain," Lafayette implored, "if you proceed with this course of action, you won't see that train we spoke of coming..."

Cordell frowned, turning back to his prisoners. "What train?"

The thing didn't have any of the comfortable familiarity that it should have.

A locomotive had come from the east toward Rubicon Crossing, impossibly, without making a rumble, sight, or sound. From the smokestack, a plume of strange green-white smoke billowed as transparent and ethereal as the cold vapour that shaped the volume of the engine and carriages that followed. It was a railroad terror usually reserved for horrific stories around the campfires of night—not the safe waking times of broad daylight.

The captain looked in time to see the ghost train arrive with speed and pass through the magician's train car. His heart pumped with fright, as did those of his soldiers. The train should have smashed everything in its path apart, mushing bodies and splintering wood and bending steel, but the thing passed through them effortlessly.

Cordell caught sight of the train's driver—what appeared to be a ghastly apparition of Charles Lafayette with burning eyes. The spectre of the magician pointed into Cordell's soul as the phantom engine passed through him, emitting a deep guttural voice from depths unknown, *"Your train is on time, Captain..."*

"That's the sign!" Jacobi forced the binoculars back to Miller." Let's move!"

CHAPTER

TWENTY-SEVEN

Around half the soldiers were panicked! Seeing a ghost train pass through their commanding officer and continue through the filed army, ignoring the physical need to stay on the railroad tracks, was certainly not an everyday comfortable military experience.

Nobody disagreed with Jacobi. Miller, Royce and Twyla both followed his sudden bold advance. The four were all unsure of what just took place on the bridge, but welcomed it as the *sign* they awaited.

Some soldiers screamed to saviours that did not respond as others found that there was more comfort over the edge of the bridge, plummeting hundreds of feet to a watery death rather than face the horror of the oncoming spectral engine.

They burst from their advantageous hiding place among the brush of a cliff edge, guns blazing, emboldened outlaws ready to rescue one of their own.

Those with the psychological mettle to withstand the terror of the oncoming apparition and those that were already more comfortable with such impossibilities took up arms in response to the ghost train and subsequent ambush. Victor switched on his gizmos, his electric suit coming alive with blinking lights and snapping sparks. The plague doctor didn't even flinch.

Hawk breathed with the relief that he was still alive after the phantom vehicle passed through him. It had knocked Cordell over with the sheer shock and unpreparedness of witnessing such an apparition before him.

"How?" Hawk asked the air, knowing all too well that there would be no answer forthcoming, "you were just...that train...was that you on the train?"

"I'm sure I don't have the foggiest of ideas as to what you are rambling on about," Lafayette ignored the question, "but it's good to see you again, Old Friend. Oh, and I do sincerely apologise for referring to you as some sort of flea-ridden common mangy prairie dog—but you must understand the nature of conversing with these repugnant men."

Hawk tapped a closed fist against his chest, smiling to the magician. "My thanks to you all the same."

Hawk and Lafayette darted behind the magician's caravan—which was untouched by the spectral train—as rifle fire began finding its way near them over the fallen army captain.

"Please, take this." Lafayette handed him one of his matching decorated guns. It was a lever-action Vulcan pistol scrawled with arcane glyphs that appeared to glow, and some crystalline ball ammunition. It was an exotic weapon by a revolver's standards, itself having no revolving cylinder and the aetron shots unable to be bought in any shop.

"Did you know, that ruckus out there is a motley crew of desperados you assembled by rescuing a young man from another part of this very river we rise above. He's leading them to your rescue. My word, how much that little boy from Boston has grown. But for our part now, make use of that weapon and let us be defiant *pistoleros*."

"It's now or never!" Jacobi shouted, raising a neckerchief over the lower half of his face. Leaving his horse behind, he charged toward the western end of Rubicon Crossing, his new revolver bursting. Everything that had happened to Jacobi since falling from that paddle steamer into the Rubicon River had led to this.

Miller and Twyla had dismounted and flanked his either side, raising their own kerchief masks over their noses, shooting their rifles at opposing soldiers. Royce had shooed Firefly away, his Holt Mustang firing between Jacobi and his flankers, adopting no mask.

Royce did not hide his face.

There was no need.

Red Roy was back!

Jacobi realised, as did his allies, that Lafayette's special ammunition was something unexpected. "Hey, our bullets are on fire!" Sure enough, each round that found its mark didn't just pierce but also burst with a small firework of chromatic sparks that scorched and burned.

Rusty took off, barking, ahead of the four. The soldiers were about to find out what it was like to be on the dog's bad side.

The panic among the soldiers flared as the ambush escalated. The opposition's ammunition exploded with lights and caught aflame as their assailants appeared with the element of surprise. Many took cover between the wagons, although the army horses attached to them tried to scramble about frantically against the wagons' braking mechanisms and what space remained on the bridge.

As soldiers closed in on the Indian and magician, Hawk and Lafayette fired in response with their matching Vulcan pistols.

Lafayette turned and ducked, only to return with his other outstretched white-gloved hand releasing decks of playing cards like springs from a novelty toy can. The cards fanned and spun and flew toward the soldiers with a preternatural precision, exploding on impact in a shower of gambled fireworks confusion.

When the soldiers were dispatched, they realised that Cordell had ascended a wagon to uncover some sort of multi-barrelled machine gun. Victor and the plague doctor joined him up there. The horses attached to the wagon were limp with blood flowing from their throats, Cordell's peculiar knife still within one of them. Hawk saw the horses, slain by the captain simply so his weapon had a steady platform.

Hawk levelled a pistol at Cordell. "You are without mercy!"

CHAPTER

TWENTY-EIGHT

Captain Cordell ducked while turning the crank of the machine gun. The contraption, already loaded, sprang to life, spitting speeding ammunition ahead of itself. Rounds pounded and bit into the magician's caravan, splintering and cracking ancient wood. As alchemical parts of the caravan exploded inside, three shots found Lafayette.

The magician dropped his fancy pistol, blood gurgling upon his goatee and moustache. The machine gun rounds had speared through his body and into his wagon.

Hawk's fists curled and he sprang forward. Any last shred of forgiveness within his spirit that he had relearned when standing over a cowering Twyla Matthias faded. A bullet grazed his shoulder from a soldier, another from the machine gun, but he lunged toward the blue-uniformed Cordell baring knuckles laced with vengeance.

Jacobi, Miller, Royce and Twyla had fought their way through the bridge but neared all too late. Rusty had mauled some soldiers, still rushing ahead.

Victor had been making things more difficult for them, firing blasts of concussive lightning that split wagons and sent burnt splinters flying. From his vantage point beside Cordell, he helped soldiers cover the rear attack.

When Royce and Victor saw each other there wasn't a moment of reunited brotherhood, but instead the intensity of their firing increased at each other. Royce made every effort to reach his brother.

Victor called from behind greasy goggles, with a confidence he usually lacked, "Witness the firepower of my *lightning accelerator*, Royce!"

The gizmologist's suit came alive with blue-white electricity. Glowing lines zapped as an arc of energy like the rung of a ladder rose between two antennae upon his back. The hissing energy coursed into a tube that was connected to the back of what looked like a poorly cobbled rifle with some blinking lights and mechanical sounds.

Victor pulled the trigger.

The weapon hissed with life.

Royce dived for cover.

He managed to dodge the electric explosion that struck right near him.

As Royce's allies took aim at the gizmologist, Victor returned electrical blasts in their direction causing them to duck for cover. Miller took the brunt of an electric shot, flying back from a snap-hiss of power.

In that moment, Royce took aim with his Holt Mustang and fired a gut shot. Although Lafayette's special ammunition struck Victor's torso, the unique leather apron the gizmologist wore absorbed all the heat and force of the firework.

Victor shot back, the lightning curling like a whip with a crack to match. Royce rolled to another wagon, but the lightning whip followed the continued guidance of Victor's gun, splintering the front of the wagon and freeing two horses.

Royce's revolver was out of ammo. Twyla had joined a recovered Miller and together—much to Miller's chagrin—they dealt with nearby soldiers.

"Nice toy, Victor!" Royce called. "You always did waste your talents."

Victor smiled. "My talents aren't wasted upon trying to spin Wyrd like you. Technology is the answer. Science! At least my talents produce something useful." The remark was accompanied by a torrent of quick lightning bursts toward Royce.

Royce looked at his gun and then produced a deck of cards. "Okay, Lady Luck, I need a favour. He shuffled the cards one-handed in his lap, then arranged them in his hand and looked over them toward Victor as though he were an opponent at a card table. "Time to tempt Fate."

Waiting for another electric whip to pass, Royce holstered his gun and stood with an outstretched hand. Victor's surroundings began to swirl in a wind, splinters of wood and other debris circled him as though he was in the eye of a miniature storm.

Royce hurdled the wagon he hid behind and closed the distance between he and his fourth half-brother. Victor had dropped his own weapon as sparks erupted from his suit of electric gizmos as splinters and iron and steel struck him.

Upon closing the gap Royce pistol-whipped his brother across the face with enough force to knock Victor unconscious. His brother fell on his front, the lens of one goggle cracking out.

The plague doctor descended the wagon toward Lafayette. "I knew this day would come, eventually, Charles Lafayette..."

The plague doctor had a woman's voice.

Charles Lafayette at once knew who it belonged to.

As did Royce.

The plague doctor, staff in belt, produced a deck of playing cards and shuffled them from hand to hand amid puffs of smoke and sparks.

Cordell changed magazines in the rotary weapon. He would try to get the machine gun going again before the Indian was on him.

Jacobi could hear the rise of a dread chorus; the clarion call of the ghost riders was nearing again. *Who was it for this time?* The weather was getting worse, storm clouds gathering at an unnatural pace, the two phenomena converging in unison. Flocks of black birds flew out from under the bridge, enveloping both sides as they flew up into the storm.

CHAPTER

TWENTY-NINE

The plague doctor removed her beaked mask.

Lafayette clutched a bullet wound. "Miss Kamiko Watanabe, my *failed* apprentice."

From afar, Royce knew who had just removed their mask. The dark hair coming down around the shoulders very familiar to him.

"I don't know *what* you are," Kamiko said, "but with all your power you refused to teach me the way of the reaver."

"Fate, M'Lass, sometimes has an ironic way of playing out. You were becoming a powerful weaver. If I had taught you such dark magics, you would have begun down the path of the reaver. If I didn't teach you, well, you have become the product of both fears.

But I, Kamiko, was not going to be responsible for your fall to darkness."

"You always did talk too much." Kamiko shuffled her cards, dealing them to herself and rearranging them. She fanned them out and they simply disappeared into a ball of green gas around her hands.

Lafayette was out of ammunition. He put his gun down to be polite. He did the same with a deck of cards but was left with hands of fire.

Kamiko motioned for the gas to surround Lafayette. The magician tried to burn it away with his own fire, but his strength had faded because of his injuries.

"Human bodies are so frail..." Charles Lafayette choked from the gas as he backed onto the balustrade of the bridge, holding his chest as blood seeped through his fingers from his shirt and vest. "My train has come. When you speak of me...speak fondly."

Cordell's crank turned with new ammunition, trying to mow down the Indian with a weapon created for attacking across a field of battle. Machine gun rounds found the caravan again and more esoteric things inside detonated.

The magician's caravan erupted in a ball of coloured fiery lightning. As the hissed cry of a cat painfully pierced all minds nearby, the blast of fireworks-like energy smashed Lafayette over the edge of the bridge to plunge hundreds of yards into the rushing waters below.

Charles Lafayette's mystery washed away with the plummeting impact and the power of the raging waters of the Rubicon River.

"No!" Miller ducked behind a wagon, reloading, then fired at whichever soldier had also fired at him. He may not have enjoyed the magician's company, but he didn't need to see him blasted away like that. Twyla took a bullet to the chest, forced to take cover with Miller. The whole scene felt like reliving the Civil War. "Fugginell, Woman, I'm not losing you too!"

"Hawk!" Jacobi had almost reached him, darting between wagons and soldiers, killing a few of the blue uniforms on the way. Adrenaline replaced any hesitation Jacobi felt—each bullet was a necessary action.

Cordell and Hawk became locked in a fistfight among some frenzied revolver fire. Jacobi only had a second to reflect upon

Lafayette's demise among the chaos before revealing the Indian's tomahawk, throwing the weapon to its owner.

It was caught.

Hawk spun with the weapon, using the flat of the blade to drop the army captain. He then held the axe-edge over Cordell's skull.

Hawk was ready to kill this relentless butcher once and for all.

As he contemplated the events around his spiritually significant tool, time seemed to slow, and his life replayed before his eyes as thunder cracked overhead.

The weather had shifted severely in an instant. Grey clouds had collected, creating what seemed like the onset of an irregular night sky forcing away the day. Over Rubicon Crossing they fell, rolling forth like a heavy fog from a broken sky.

The ghost riders.

They were here.

Jacobi shouted as rain fell across the area and Miller, Royce and Twyla arrived. "Surely you're seeing them this time?" he said to Royce. As the former Bostonian turned away, the scars on his face from the Trikuhl glowed like the embers of mythical brimstone, the scars of his body trying to shine through his western clothing. Jacobi gave Hawk ballistic cover, revolver with firework rounds in hand.

Royce was seeing them.

At long last, he was seeing *them*.

He was seeing all of it. All of *them*. He was finally witnessing the ghastly visage of the ghost riders.

And it scared the living daylights out of him. "Fuggsake. Holy shid!" Royce was tempered against the supernatural things of the West, but these spirits spoke right into his heart, calling his name and offering a moment of redemption.

"Fugg me," Miller gasped, "his hair's turned white." Then he looked knowingly to Jacobi. "Royce's hair turned white."

"I always said it was white!"

Twyla couldn't believe it. "Yeah, just you, but now we're all seeing it white."

"It's not me..." Jacobi understood something, something intangible—seeing it, sensing it—almost as though the ineffable Web of Fate could actually be tangible. "It's you...Royce...the threads of *Fate* have been trying to warn you about the impulsive path you travel, the reckless life you lead. They've always been with you, trying to reach you, but others have needed to see them for you because you ignore the signs. Until now. Everything has changed. It's all connected."

Rusty pounced at a soldier, growling with dripping fangs, his fur like spines of fire, eyes like hot glowing coals. He tore shreds of flesh and blue uniform, soldiers screaming of a "Hellhound!" The dog pounced about the bridge with a preternatural agility appearing as a beast from Below.

A bullet knocked Twyla's bonnet off while another found its purchase in her chest again. Instead of screaming with pain, the tomahawk wound upon her usually porcelain scalp spewed with a hot red light from a place nobody dared to know. She stood up from her place, emboldened by the meteorological arrival of the ghost riders, to unleash a torrent of exploding ammunition back upon the attacking soldiers.

Miller sprang away, getting a group of soldiers on the run westward along the bridge. The veteran's coat burned with fire, transforming it grey. Another fire reformed the coat to blue. A third fire returned his coat to that of the outlaw trapper he had become.

His eyes burned with the raging fires of war, his entire body smouldering with a smoke from Beyond.

As Hawk held Cordell, pinned under the tomahawk upon his skull, the Indian heard a wave of rolling thunder followed by the unrelenting cracking of a storm. A giant bird, the likes of which he hadn't seen in his visions for years, swooped with a group of the ghastly ghost riders from the East flying West. The colossal bird shook its massive head, lightning shooting from its eyes into the Indian. Chortling with the sound of a thunderstorm, it flew straight into Hawk's chest where it had once been painted, disappearing with a snap-hiss of sparks.

Jacobi needed to know from Royce. "You saw that, right, that giant bird just flew into Hawk...with the others out there, you can still see all this, right?"

"I do." Royce smiled to Jacobi as Hawk's eyes swirled with snapping sparks. "And I see *Jacobi-Nicholson-no-more,* instead an *Outlaw of the West*, you whom *Fate* weaved into this, leading us all to the here-and-now, in defiance of those who do not respect the West."

Just as his soldiers were, Captain Cordell was also witnessing the terrifying apparitions. "Get off me! What is this?" Despite a familiarity to such unnatural things, fear still gripped the wounded army captain. Fear, and outrage at the defiance of these criminals.

"You'll be executed as an outlaw if you don't shoot this savage off me now!" Cordell still tried to free himself while barking at Jacobi. "Who do you think you are, helping this prairie dog?"

Jacobi studied the necklace Hawk had given him when they first met: the whittled wood fashioned like a mix between a snowflake and a spider's web. "Good question." Jacobi knew what he had become in this Wild West, this *Wyrd Wild West*, giving Cordell the answer that *Fate* had led him to.

"I'm Jac...I am *Jack*...Jack the Outlaw..." He raised his arms to draw attention to the spirits swirling about the bridge. "And we here...we are *ghost riders!*"

Hawk felt a unifying sensation from the thunder that followed Jacobi's words—from this new *Jack*. These spectral beings had presented a moral choice each time they appeared to an individual, but this time those past witnesses had become their metaphysical extensions.

"And I..." the Indian looked to Jack, knowing that he would know of the stories by now, "I am *Thunder Hawk*...Spiritwalker of the Takoda...Spiritwalker of the Horse Nation!"

Thunder Hawk's face became a skull, his long hair waves of fire. "We are ghost riders," he waved his tomahawk around at the immaterial riders and their living counterparts, "and we will decide your Fate."

To stop him escaping, Thunder Hawk sunk his tomahawk blade into Cordell's leg rather than his head. As the soldier screamed, the Indian used the same ropes that had bound him during his forced march from Sundown to tie him to the balustrade of Rubicon Crossing where Lafayette had fallen.

After losing more soldiers, morale was low among the army. Those that could, fled their leader. Jack Nicholson, Alfred Miller, Royce Falco, Twyla Matthias and Rusty came before Thunder Hawk and a tethered Cordell while continuing to return fire upon any remaining soldiers. Their terrifying veneers mocked him. Each one had the means—and most the motive—to kill the captain and it tore apart his ego that he was at their mercy.

"Betrayer." He acknowledged Twyla Matthias. "How could you have fallen in with such a lot? We would have had everything. *Qonkura* rewards those who conquer."

She didn't know who or what clandestine thing he referred to. She nodded to Jacobi, "I would rather fall in line with this *posse* than continue to fall as far as you have. The terrible things you have done. The terrible things *we* have done."

Royce tried to lighten the mood, "I think were more of a *gaggle* than a posse."

Cordell faced Jacobi. "Beware of the path you are walking, *Jack the Outlaw.*" The Captain's stare bore right into his soul. "Heed my warning and turn back from this reckless posse now or suffer your doom. *Thus is Fate.*"

"Take your Sicarius Assembly and shove it up your arrz!" Despite her wounds, Twyla punched Cordell across the face. Their enemy fell unconscious. "Now that's how you hit somebody properly," she explained to Miller.

Jack whooped while pondering Cordell's mysterious words as Twyla shook her aching fist.

Royce was the first to notice. "Where's Kamiko gone? She's got a lot to answer for."

"I don't know," Miller answered. "And that bidge has got a lot to pay for. She just...disappeared somehow...in the chaos."

Kuhl-kuhl-kuhl...

Jacobi had heard that noise before.
That call.
The call of a Trikuhl.

"Shiiiiiid..." Royce also knew all too well what was approaching. "We're not out of this yet."

Miller caught Royce's worried gaze. "How are we supposed to deal with this without Lafayette?" the veteran breathed.

It didn't matter where Kamiko Watanaba vanished to, there was something more sinister coming.

The thing rose from under the bridge, spiderlike with each step of its black skeletal limbs. The impossible creature emanated a black mist that seemed to shroud it in a camouflage that made parts of it disappear and reappear from sight.

It was a beast that fuelled nightmares, a thing that should not be, a terror under the canopy of the storm and ghost riders and corvids.

Twyla gasped, tugging Miller's arm. "What is that thing?"

They heard the monster respond in their minds. *Con'kooh'rah.*

Jacobi somehow, in some way, understood it: "*Qonkura.*"

CHAPTER

✦

THIRTY

Twyla grabbed Cordell's military saber. "The *cap* won't miss this right now."

"*Kuhl-kuhl-kuhl,*" the monster uttered, this time heard with the ears, a chittering sound that drove up the spines of those that suffered it.

This thing was beyond the words and images of Jacobi's dime stories.
Beyond his worst dreams.
The thing was bigger than a human, both physical and unreal at the same time, a mass of shadow and gaunt limbs. If an accurate count could be had, there were nine skeletal limbs, eight of the spider-like legs and one limb that curved up behind like a scorpion's

tail with a tipped stinger. Three sets of three red eyes seemed to watch the posse all at once, all present under the monster's fearful gaze. It climbed like an arachnid before them, but stood like both an arachnid and a human being.

And the thing was marked.

Wounded.

This was the monster that Jacobi was nearly taken by in Rubicon River when he fell from the steamer.

There were places along the dark exoskeletal limbs that weren't perfect. Recovered areas that had been hit by bullets fired from the River Grace.

And a grievously damaged eye...

Qonkura—this Trikuhl creature—had tried to capture and devour Jacobi. It had skittered about Twyla Matthias for who knows how long and phased around Kamiko Watanabe.

If Royce feared the thing he didn't show it. "So you're *Qonkura*, a godhead of the Sicarius Assembly. Well...all I see is 'gater bait."

He holstered his gun. Withdrew a deck of cards and shuffled them quickly and vigorously. When he was finished he held the collection whole, clenched in one hand. Light shone from the deck toward the Trikuhl.

A light that the monster despised.

"Now!" Royce commanded.

Miller fired his rifle as many times as he could.

Jacobi let loose with his revolver.

Twyla drew her own saber and took to the creature, dual-wielding like she was from the pages of one of Jacobi's story books.

Thunder Hawk was upon it, fearless, tomahawk repeatedly cutting into any limbs that came near him, spilling emerald blood.

The creature reacted, screeching. Nobody could tell if the Trikuhl was blinded by Royce's light, but it certainly had made an opening for the posse to attack.

Many bullets found their mark and sabers cut into limbs.

The Trikhul responded, the scorpion-like stinger tail coming down through Royce's deck of cards and into his chest.

Royce's magic light went out.

So did Royce.

The veins of his face went black.

"Sunnuvabidge!" Miller charged the creature as Royce went down.

"Not you too," Twyla cried out for Royce as she and Hawk were swept aside by a bludgeoning spider-limb.

Jacobi ran out of Lafayette's aetron bullets. Was it was time to use the forbidden cards that Royce had given him in the stagecoach?

Twyla and Hawk smashed into Miller as he tried to use the butt of his rifle as a weapon. The veteran managed to fly away farther than the pair did, the ex-Gold Baroness and Indian falling at the creature's feet.

"Hey, Qonkura," Royce had crawled his way in pain to where his brother had fallen goggles-down on the bridge under him. His face had become a web of dark lines, some form of venom coursing through him. Royce had pried the cobbled gun of the lightning accelerator from Victor's unconscious hands, aimed at the Trikuhl and fired.

The burst of electrical energy unfurled like the end of a cracking whip upon the shadowy beast. The monster reeled back.

Twyla stabbed a saber into the thing from underneath it's arachnid form, releasing a screech that pierced their ears.

Hawk kept the tomahawk attacking, finding flesh and exoskeleton to break.

Miller was upon the wagon with the rotary machine gun. He'd put in a new magazine and turned the crank. Powerful bulletheads chewed into the Trikuhl.

Twyla stabbed the other saber into the monster.

Royce switched to a rapid fire mode that kept a constant pumping of electric shots going at the monster.

But it wasn't enough.

The beast was too powerful.

Until Royce told Jacobi it was, "Time to spin Wyrd!"

The young man took everything he'd learned about magic from Charles Lafayette and Royce Falco and shuffled it into his deck. "If there was ever a time to *tempt* Fate, this is it."

He held the deck of cards out in his left hand and skimmed each card from the top in succession. The cards were like bullets, flying into the monster and striking with an explosive force like they were some of Lafayette's magical ammunition.

Electrical blasts.

Saber piercings.

Tomahawk cuts.

Rotary machine gun bullets.

With the additional magic of Jacobi's exploding Wyrd, the barrage of varied attacks was enough to force the creature to the rail.

From what could only be described as dark three-fingered skeletal hands, a silver line was shot from two palms, each finding a purchase upon the wood of the bridge to halt the Trikuhl's forced movement.

It was two lines of strong sticky web.

But a tomahawk cut one.

And explosive cards burned the other.

The final nail in the monster's coffin was the barging attack of Rusty, the dog using its body to slam into the monster, finally toppling the Trikuhl from the heights of the bridge.

As the Trikuhl fell from the heavens of Rubicon Crossing to the smashing depths of Rubicon River below, the spectral riders surrounding began to fade away, as did the hellish guises of the outlaws.

Reunited with the husky as his usual red and white furred self, Rusty became the focus of many warm greetings.

"Fugg me, that was brutal!" Miller was looking north-east through his binoculars. "But there's no time to waste. Reinforcements from Fort Morgan are riding in fast. They're probably wondering where Cordell and his prisoner are. We gotta go now. I doubt we'll get a second chance."

"We need to search for Lafayette's body," Twyla interrupted, waving at the charred remains of the magician's caravan.

"Chuck's gone." Miller had to hide the water in his eyes. "Nobody falls from Rubicon Crossing and lives to talk about it. He's 'gator bait now, along with that Trikuhl."

It was difficult to accept for all of them, but Charles Lafayette was gone—and they all heard the dying feline hiss of his cat, Memphis, in their minds.

"What about Royce?" Twyla asked, looking at what had happened to his face and hair. The man's veins were black and thick from the Trikuhl venom and his hair white from fright.

With the voice of wisdom, Thunder Hawk assisted Royce. "We go now, or we all die. I will ask Great Spirit for mercy upon my brother."

Jack called, firing at some remaining soldiers. "Alright then, we've got our prisoner and a patient. Let's get out of here!"

"We'll need to hide for a while until all this passes," Thunder Hawk stated. "Cordell can wake up to the Fate of his own moral compass, as we've all had to do in the past. I'm sorry that my need for vengeance brought you all into this mess, but we may as well stay together for now."

"Twyla put it well before," Jack added.

"Put what well?" Miller's brow raised.

"We're a *posse*...that's what we've become."

"Like I said," Royce reminded, "I think were more of a gaggle."

"Oh no," Jacobi nodded, "we're a posse!"

"Yep." Miller dropped the binoculars around his neck. "I'll ride with this posse any day."

They hadn't realised it until this moment, but that's exactly what they had become.

A posse.

CHAPTER

THIRTY-ONE

As the outlaws fought their way through straggling soldiers from Rubicon Crossing to their horses, Thunder Hawk caught sight of a familiar black domestic cat prancing casually over a rocky outcropping. "Is that...?"

The cat paused, regally, noting the posse, then disappeared into the brush.

"Is *that*, what?" Miller asked.

"Nothing..." Thunder Hawk smiled to himself. "It'd only annoy you."

"Are you all enigmatic again now?" Royce laughed. "People, *Thunder Hawk* has returned!"

THUNDER ROAD

They would ride together with haste out of there, Rusty running faithfully alongside. The constant threat of the pursuing army would be like lighting striking behind them. They were going to ride faster and farther than any of them had ever rode before.

Jack pointed as far West as possible into the setting sun. "Okay, *posse*, let's ride this Thunder Road!"

Kamiko Watanabe peered from the safety of an eastern cliff edge. She witnessed her former allies slay a Trikuhl—a feat she thought impossible. Placing her beaked mask on, she watched them escape.

Jack accepted that Fate had bound them together in ways he was only beginning to understand within the Mysterium that Lafayette had spoken of. They were outlaws of the West now, riding the Thunder Road.

A nameless posse.

Or...were they?

EPILOGUE

BOUND BY FATE

"Let the Lady go…"

It was almost midnight. Elizabeth would never dream of roaming Sundown after dark unless it was absolutely necessary. She needed to find which saloon her Father was inside because one of their horses was about to give birth. She'd managed to politely avoid the many grubby hands in Sundowner Saloon and was moving on to try at the Pig and Swig, but the persistent reaching of one young man had followed her despite her many refusals.

A shadowy visage took the pursuer and the pursued by surprise. It suddenly appeared ahead of them in an alleyway full of piled crates that Elizabeth had attempted to lose the young man through. Under the poor starlight, the tilted brim of a hat hid most of the shadowy visage's features. Only a scarred jaw of stubble revealed the mouth that had given the command. Its hands were loose, jacket slightly revealing a holstered revolver.

"Get out of here, Mister," the pursuer slurred, "she's with me."

"No, I'm not." Elizabeth used the moment to move away. "I'm not with him at all. I'm trying to find my father."

"Francis Geddes..." The shadowy visage knew the name of the woman's pursuer, its breath a ghostly white against the cold night. "Let the Lady go or be damned to ride for eternity among us." As he spoke, it was as though a shallow fog rolled from behind him through the alleyway.

Francis had drunk too much.

Again.

Despite the stroke of good luck that had freed him from the servitude of the mines of Boom Town, his personality was always his own worst enemy. It was only a matter of time before his incessant voice and actions landed him in another hazardous situation like the one that had happened aboard the *River Grace*.

"No, she's mine!" Francis stumbled, trying to put on a gruff exterior. "And how do you know my name?"

An arrow shot from behind the shadowy visage, piercing Francis by his shirt to a stacked wooden crate.

Elizabeth didn't know what to do. "Thank you. Thank you, Mister. I'll go now. I'll go." She counted her blessings and headed back out of the alley, heading home instead of chancing another Sundown night encounter. Damn her father—she decided to take care of the birth herself.

"Francis Geddes," the shadowy visage said again, tossing a leather pouch. "Go Back East. Leave the Wild West. Or ride with us...forevermore."

The bag clinked as it landed at Francis' feet. It sounded hefty—full of coins. "With us? How do you know...? There's only you. Who are you?"

A lantern came to life as Francis tore his shirt to lean down for the bag, freeing himself.

A group had been waiting silently in the night. A dark brown horse with white blaze stood riderless behind the shadowy visage. Farther behind, a weathered man with greying beard held the lantern atop a grey horse. A woman bearing a deep scar across her forehead sat side-saddle upon a brown and white steed. A man with wild white hair held a large revolver across his shoulder as he sat upon a horse with a red coat. Another man with long black hair held an antler bow aimed with an arrow upon a golden-tan steed with tiger stripes. A red husky with peculiar eyes groaned with ill will toward Francis while a smooth black cat—eyes yellow—crossed between him and the shadowy visage.

Jack—the shadowy visage—doffed his hat, Francis fleeing into the night toward the train station from the answer.

"Who are we...? We're the Ghost Riders!"

ABOUT THE AUTHOR

Luke Tracey lives in Brisbane, Queensland, Australia. He holds a Bachelor of Arts in Communication Studies. Growing up he was fascinated by Native American culture and spirituality and the history of what was considered the Wild West era of America. Books like *Bury My Heart at Wounded Knee* by Dee Brown and documentaries such as *The West* and *The Civil War* by Ken Burns kept that fascination alive. And later, video games such as *Red Dead Redemption* and *Red Dead Redemption II* would spark the idea of creating an alternate history of the Wild West. An avid fan of pop culture, characters such as Superman, Spider-Man, Luke Skywalker and Optimus Prime have inspired his idea of what it means to be a hero. Luke has even put on Star Wars costumes and become Spider-Man or a Ghostbuster at pop culture conventions and charity events. Luke considers himself a "*Wyrdo*" and it is his fond hope that his stories inspire readers to spin their own kind of Wyrd.

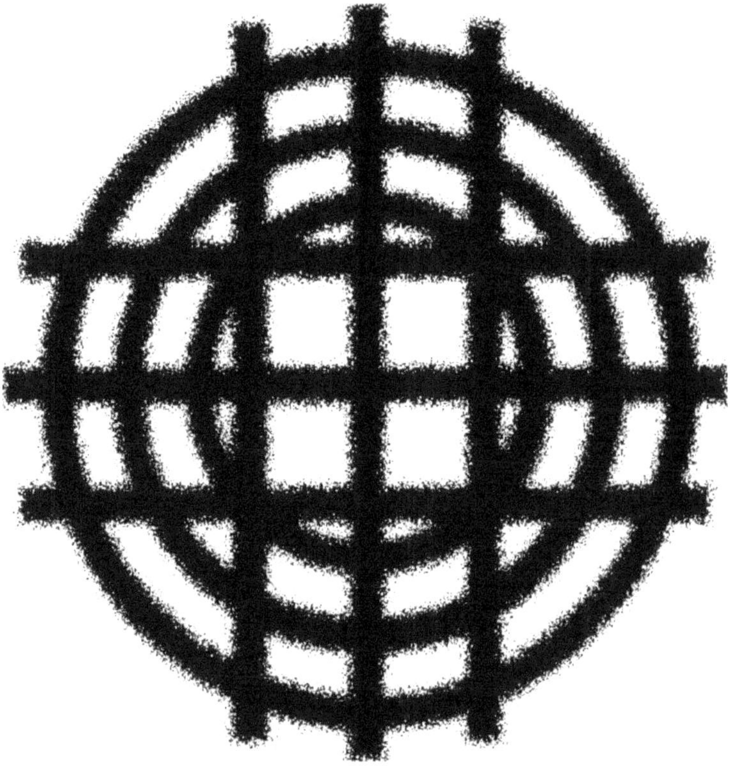

www.ingramcontent.com/pod-product-compliance
Ingram Content Group UK Ltd.
Pitfield, Milton Keynes, MK11 3LW, UK
UKHW041854250225
455528UK00006B/30